A Barksin Book
Produced by Nadir Catalano

Illustrations by Rory Midhani

Design: Peterman Studio, Milan
Layout: Alexandra Gredler
Editor: Sarah Goodrum

Paperback ISBN 978-3-9821270-1-9
E-book ISBN 978-3-9821270-2-6

www.gwennaluna.com

THE DARK BOOK OF GWENNA LUNA

GUENTHER PRIMIG

SIX DREAMS OF THE SUPERNATURAL

"They had ghosts as real as ever there were, superstition was rife, the wise woman was fresh in their memory. . . . Parishioners said there always were witches, and always would be."

Catherine E. Parsons, Folklorist,
Cambridgeshire Lecture

"Evil betide me if I do not open the door to know if that is true which is said concerning it. So he opened the door . . . and when they had looked they were conscious of all the evils they had ever sustained, and of all the friends and companions they had lost and of all the misery that had befallen them, as if it had happened on that very spot; . . . and because of their perturbation they could not rest."

David Jones,
In Parentheses

WEST MEDFORD, MA, 4 pm

She didn't sound like the type of patient he usually saw. Gwenna Luna. A strange name. Age: Seventeen. He was, he admitted to himself, a little curious about this one. Patients that age needed saving, the years and years before them at stake.

Wilson had been in practice fifteen years. He prospered on the worried well, a wealthy clientele old enough to feel a slight thrill of ennoblement at undergoing therapy with a black doctor. Saving hadn't had anything to do with it for years.

His town was ideal: a liberal, prosperous Boston suburb. He did well by his patients. What they wanted was a kind ear and little pills. Little pills he had aplenty. He distributed them by playing a game he called Prescription Bingo: Key words scored points for team paranoia, team depression, or team anxiety, and as his patients talked he pictured little race horses, moving ahead, falling behind, until a lucky winner emerged and his prescription pad came out. From the point of view of a medical board, the game might be considered a little frivolous. But those were his cases, those were his patients. His was the sort of practice where prescription bingo made perfect sense. Nobody got hurt.

And now—Gwenna Luna. Seventeen.

A strange name.

1

"*Gwenna Luna is here, Doctor.*"

"*Thanks.*"

Sadie lingered in the door. Something in her face confirmed Wilson's intuition: Whoever had followed that name into his waiting room was unusual.

"*She didn't give an address,*" *Sadie said.* "*And she doesn't seem to have insurance.*"

Wilson leaned back in his chair.

"*Well,*" *he said.* "*Let's have a look. We'll have a little chat.*"

Sadie stepped aside, and the girl came in without making a sound.

She was a slight girl, only her flowing clothes giving her, it seemed, any substance at all. Her hair was short, chopped carelessly, and Wilson felt sure that she had done it herself. He noticed a paleness, a near translucence that was ghostly. He also caught a glimpse of razor blade cuts. The scars came down to the girl's wrists, and he suspected that they ran the length of her arms under the wide sleeves. There was a piercing in her upper lip that looked new enough for a slight swelling, and she had a childlike way of moving her lower lip over it, gnawing, as she surveyed his office.

A young, pale, pained, quiet mess, he thought, not without sympathy. Then she looked at him, and he saw an excitement in her eyes. She seemed filled with an inner triumph so inexplicable and at odds with her appearance, he already felt he had gotten his money's worth. She completed this strange impression by saying, in a light, pretty voice: "*There you are!*"

Wilson looked at Sadie.

Sadie looked at Wilson.

"*Well,*" *Wilson said,* "*I guess here I am, yes.*"

He noticed the cloth bag the girl wore over her shoulder. "*Salisbury Home Savings.*"

"*Will you...*" *Sadie started.*

"*Oh, yes,*" *Wilson said.* "*Hold my calls.*"

"*What do I put on the insurance form?*"

"*We'll have a talk first,*" *Wilson said. He nodded at Sadie and she withdrew, closing the door behind her.*

The girl's eyes followed her out, then turned back to Wilson. There was an intention there, he felt. She had a definite purpose.

"*Sit down,*" *Wilson said, finding it, somehow, necessary to declare the upper hand.*

She slid into a chair.

"*Relax,*" *he said,* "*We're just chatting now. You're not in therapy, yet.*"

"You help people?" she asked abruptly.

He kept a straight face.

"When I can."

"That's what I want," she said, nodding. There it was again, that sense of purpose.

He caught a glimpse of her scars again and thought of his sister. His sister, at that age, the only black kid in a school of rich bullies. His sister, who called him once a week, suggesting trips and visits. His sister, whom nobody had saved at seventeen and whose calls he usually avoided.

"Where's your mother?" he asked.

Quickly, Gwenna Luna ran her teeth over her piercing. She had a tell, then.

"That's a good question," she said.

"I thought she called for your appointment."

"No, I called myself."

"I see," he said quietly. "Help."

She turned solemn.

"Yes," she said. "Help."

All her hope was in that word. She caressed it.

They sat facing each other for a moment, in agreement.

"Well," Wilson said. "What do we do? I can't treat you without your parents' consent and without insurance. In fact, I should call child protective services, have you picked up."

"Just write down I'm twenty-one," she said.

She only maintained the brashness of her answer for a moment, until a gust of wind rattled the window. There was a quick, almost instant change in her, a flash of instinctual bravery in the face of fear. The fear, Wilson realized, was always present, sometimes apparently present enough to make her cut and bleed.

"It's fall," Wilson said. "Just the wind."

She kept looking at the window, expecting he didn't know what. She said the next thing quietly, almost to herself.

"My mother was a witch."

The light seemed to drain from the office. The weather was changing.

"She came from Bulgaria, the Stranja mountains. My father brought her here. A few years ago, she disappeared. She was a witch."

Then, reluctantly: "She is a witch."

Wilson put down his notebook.

"Is that who you're afraid of?" he asked calmly.

She didn't answer. He turned on his desk lamp, and a warm glow filled the office. Shadows banished. There were drugs that would do the same for her mind, he thought.

Help...

"So why do you come to me?" he asked. His voice was steady and without judgment. "I'm not Doctor Freud. I don't care about your mother."

She gave him a look that meant not caring about her mother might be a terrible mistake.

Wilson had heard of the Stranja mountains. That was a place where weird things happened, a place where whole villages moved because of voices from the woods. A childhood, then, filled with superstitious dread.

"I have a plan," Gwenna Luna said. "Do you want to hear it?"

"Tell me."

She reached into her bag and brought out what looked like an old diary.

"After mother left, I found one of her books. It was in the basement of our house. She had several of them. She must have lost this one when she ran away."

She opened the book, and Wilson saw pages and pages covered in writing, some of it in English, some in Cyrillic letters. There were symbols, too, and numbers.

"A book of . . ."

"Spells," said the girl. "It's one of her books of spells."

"Spells," Wilson said.

The girl paused, realizing, perhaps, that her eagerness had made her careless. She watched him for a moment.

"You talk, I listen," Wilson said, reassuringly.

He thought that she would comfortably win every game of prescription bingo ever played.

He decided to draw her out.

"Can you do . . . spells? You perform them?"

She shook her head.

"Not yet," she said. "I haven't translated them, not completely. I'm still learning. Some of the letters are strange."

"Those are Cyrillic," Wilson said.

"Those are not the ones I mean," said Gwenna Luna.

"Your mother knew how."

"Oh, yes," said Gwenna Luna. "Mother knew how."

She was so lost in these delusions. They had been, Wilson realized, bred into her.

"That plan you have," he said. "Tell me about it."

She was silent for a while.

"There's a lot of things to be afraid of," she finally said. "There's a lot of horrible things to be afraid of. I want to stop something. I want to save someone. I want to know I did some good, have a use. I want to say to myself, just once: "Bam. Good witch.""

Wilson saw a line of text in the book still open on the table, something about the raising of demons.

"You want to fight the monsters?" he asked.

A childhood like that. He realized her intense loneliness, understood her immense need. To be a hero.

"Do you have friends?" he asked gently.

She ran her hand across the book of spells and looked up at him, as if the question had never occurred to her.

"Not yet," she said.

There was so much work to do, Wilson thought. There was a whole series of articles in this. He would help her. He would never be bored again. He couldn't wait to begin.

"That's your plan, then," he said. "Now. What made you come to me?"

The darkness slid over her face again. From her glorious future, it was back to the fear. He could see her plan: cutting off her hair, a new piercing, a new person.

Find, he told himself, what made her run.

"Why did you come to see me?" he pushed.

"The dreams," she said.

He waited.

"The dreams that aren't dreams," she said.

"Dreams," Wilson said, "are a good place to start."

She looked at him straight, and there was a change in her. She seemed, suddenly, much older, a shape by the roadside beckoning him into danger.

"I have the same dream, for a time, over and over," she said. "And it's not a dream, really. I'm somebody else. I experience, completely, something that happened to somebody else."

"Somebody you know?"

"No."

"But you think these people are real?" Wilson asked.

"I researched them. Some of these things happened a long time ago. Some recently. But they happened. Exactly in the way I dreamed them."

"What sort of things happened?" Wilson asked.

He was fascinated by the change in her.

Her eyes were full of ancient danger.

"Strange things," she said.

Stories of the Stranja mountains.

The raising of demons.

Mother knew how.

Cut. Cut. Cut.

He leaned back.

"What do you think," he asked, "we should do about those dreams?"

She checked the window again, and he thought about closing the blinds. The window distracted her. She seemed to expect a face to appear there.

"I want to show you," she said.

"Show me?"

She reached for her bag again. For a moment Wilson expected, absurdly, that she would produce something grotesque—a human heart, a severed ear. He shrank back. What she placed on his desk was a black spiral notebook.

"Another book?" Wilson said.

"This one's mine," said Gwenna Luna.

"You write down your dreams?"

She shook her head, slowly.

"What are you going to show me?" Wilson asked.

She watched him steadily. He could tell she had come to the point, the purpose she carried with her. It was the moment she decided to jump and for one moment there was the frightened seventeen-year-old girl again.

"There's an old man, he lives in a monastery," said Gwenna Luna. "Every time a cloud passes and the sunlight fades, he's so afraid that he cries. I dreamed what happened to him. Then I found him."

She opened the book.

There were crude drawings. At first, they looked like dabs of ink and short, unconnected lines, a mad alphabet. Then they became clearer. Shapes began to emerge, figures. They were like cave paintings, simple but full of movement. Wilson recognized, suddenly, severed arms, heads. There was, he thought, a bent human figure holding an immense ax.

"Do you see it?" she asked. "Do you?"

"What is this?" Wilson said.

The pictures began to move . . .

"You see it," she said, with immense relief. "Don't look away."

It felt like falling. He was an old man hiding in a monastery, remembering what happened. The strange things. It felt like falling, and then he was a young man . . .

THE
COACHMAN

There were four of us. Me, Roberts, Harry and, of course, Clayton. Four American boys done with school. In those days, kings of the world.

Off to Europe we went, with more money than was good for us. Serious debauchery—we boozed and fornicated our way up the Italian boot. Clayton almost got arrested in the Vatican. A one-eyed priest called him a "damned boy," and it was only later I realized he had meant it in a spiritual sense and not, as we laughingly thought, as a clumsy attempt to curse in American.

We reached the top of the boot before vacation was over. We had three weeks left and no idea where to go. At a train station, we got a tip to go across the mountains. So we just kept going, across the border and into Austria. We stepped off the train in a place called Klagenfurt: a city situated next to a lake we were assured was just the thing for tourists. Outside the city limits it was an old place, peasant country. A place where people are afraid of ghosts. Not telling stories about them, not believing in them in some abstract fashion. That's a pleasant shudder around a fire. The country people, in those days, knew real fear, and that's a very different thing.

The city itself is over seven hundred years old, and most of the old houses in the center are still standing.

Not that the four of us cared about those things. We were tired. Italy had worn us out. So we bought some cases of booze and rented a small shack outside the city, out on the swampy meadows around the lake. The place was like a moor, really, with very soggy ground. But you woke up to see the lake out the front door, and there weren't any neighbors to bother you.

At night, you could see the city at a distance. And if you turned and looked in the other direction, you saw the moor. And those lights. Odd lights, green and blue, dancing in the dark. I began to feel queer about the place then, that first night. I don't know about the others, but I looked at those lights and there was something timeless about them. You can call them swamp gas all you want. But I didn't like them at all.

For three days, we didn't leave our shack on the moor. We spent the days drinking, swimming, and sleeping. The days were beautiful—warm, dry summer heat and the water cold and deep and so clear you could see fish all the way at the bottom, fish so huge they must have come with the beginning of the lake.

By the end of the fourth day, all of us were a little tired of doing nothing. Roberts started looking through the cabin. A lot of junk accumulates in a place that's been rented out over the years. He found this odd little book, sort of a history of the place. It was a shabby old thing, printed, I think, sometime in the thirties. The cover was missing, the pages stiff as cardboard, and it had a horrible smell to it. The odd thing was, it was in English. I don't remember any of the stories in that book, folk legends collected in the area. I only glanced at it. Stories about dragons in the moor and angry dwarves drowning cities for their sins.

But one story I do remember. Roberts read it to us that night, the fourth night at the cabin. It was the story of the Coachman.

There was a very rich man, living in the city. This was around fourteen-thirty-something—I remember thinking that it was some time before Columbus. The book still spelled the name of the city as Clagenfurth, and just looking at that spelling you saw ancient mists over the lake.

Anyway, this very rich man built a moderate estate on the moors, directly by the lake. His purpose was to establish a small group of fishermen and their families to supply the city on market days and make a profit doing it. In this man's employ, from many years earlier, was a coachman. He was the most trusted servant of the household, a man who worked magic with horses. His master was absurdly fond of the animals, and this had been the early connection between the two that now led to the coachman's advancement.

He was given a house on the moor and was charged with overseeing the fishermen. He became his master's eyes and ears. And a solid, honest man he seemed to be. He never drank, never gambled. He saw to the transport of the fish and reported on the conduct and morals of the outpost. He was, then, at the beginning of the story, no longer just a simple servant.

In fact, the coachman became something of a ruler over the six households by the lake. After a year, his master became ill, and the coachman's power grew. Little direction came his way from the city. As long as the fish arrived in time for Thursday's market, he was left alone and was never questioned.

He began to turn strange. He left his house for a small cabin that he built further into the moor. He dug a pit next to the cabin that filled with warm mud oozing out of the ground like the blood of the earth. The coachman was seen to bathe in it. At night, he would sit in the hole, talking as he wallowed in the mud. He held real conversations, with pauses allowed for responses nobody else could hear.

The families living on the estate were concerned. But they did not suspect any outright danger, not until the first girl vanished. She was fifteen—the most beautiful girl living on the moor, to be married the next spring. She had left her friends one evening, and from the way she smiled they were sure she had arranged to meet the boy she was to marry.

She was presumed drowned, not an uncommon occurrence in fishing communities. But two months later, a second girl disappeared without a trace. And a mere two days later, a third. The second was one of the friends left behind that evening when the first girl walked into oblivion. The third was merely visiting relatives. At nineteen, she was the oldest.

Panic ensued. The families left without packing after that third girl. They rushed to the city, food still sitting on the tables in their houses.

When the authorities came for the coachman—for his strange behavior of the previous months had been reported—they expected to find that he'd gone. But he sat in front of his cabin, calmly smoking a pipe. He didn't speak, ask any questions, or defend himself in any way. He went peacefully.

This is what he confessed under torture:

He had seduced the girls. He had them bathe in the hole of mud by his cabin, at night. Then he split their heads with an ax and chopped their bodies into pieces. Pieces small as little mice, he said. He left them there, in the mud, to bathe in, and to bathe his new victims as their turns came.

There were two things about the coachman's confession that horrified the city. The first was that the confession, extracted under torture, was not given with screams and sobs of pain. He had been oblivious to the cruelest methods of interrogation. He had flung his confession at them, laughing and telling them to go and look into that mud hole. And to look deep.

That led to the discovery of the second peculiarity: In that hole there were found far more pieces of dismembered bodies than could be accounted for with the missing girls. It is said that there were enough bones to make at least twenty humans—men, women and children, intermingled with the small bones of animals, some of them unidentifiable and utterly grotesque.

The coachman was drawn and quartered in the town square. His house was burned to the ground.

That's the story as Roberts read it that night. Our reaction to it was predictable. From some references to the lake shore in the account, we concluded that the Coachman's crimes had occurred in the very area where we had taken our cabin. It seemed unchanged from centuries ago—still a moor, lights still dancing at night. We were drunk and stupid, and it was late and it was dark outside. Of course, we went to look for the place.

We took our flashlights and followed Roberts, who carried the book. There was a good deal of laughing and joking as we set out. Not so much later. We stumbled around on that moor, finding absolutely nothing, laughing if one of us stepped into a bog and sank up to his knees, stopping now and then to relieve ourselves.

After two hours or so, the joke had gone stale. I remember clearly that it was Clayton who gave our search a new direction. He had the idea, just as we were about to head for home. He sat in the grass, and he turned off his flashlight. We stopped, turning ours off, too. And Clayton pointed to where the moor lights were dancing.

"What if that's the Coachman, over there?" he said.

We set off in the dark, after those lights.

After fifteen minutes we ran into the stones.

We all stopped, looking at them. There was no mistaking it: Overgrown as they were, they could form nothing but the foundation of a house.

At once, we turned on our lights. We looked at the stones, and nobody said anything; and all the frogs in that bog croaked on and on, as always.

Roberts called out, "Look at this! Over here!"

We followed his light with ours. There was a depression in the ground. It looked like a bowl, six feet across, covered with grass and dead leaves.

The depression was slight, now, but it had clearly been much deeper once. It was just a scar now. Unnatural looking. It was right next to where the house once stood.

I wasn't sure whether to laugh or not. It was funny, us stumbling across the moor on this drunken lark, looking for this storybook house of horrors. To find a site so fitting in all particulars. My God—it was probably some hunter's cabin, but I thought it was a great joke, in any case.

Well, Clayton had no difficulty deciding on a reaction. He laughed. Like this was the best joke he'd ever heard. That broke the spell for the rest of us. At once we reverted to ignorant, loud, drunken boys.

That's when we did it. The unforgivable. It was a joke, nothing more. We had pulled dozens like it all through that summer.

Harry started it, by making an eerie sound. A really bad ghost sound is what it was. And I laughed, and said:

"You've done it, Clayton. You've found the Coachman's house. What now? You wanna take a bath?"

I should have died before I said it.

Harry kept up that stupid sound, holding his flashlight under his chin like a child. And we all started crowding Clayton and Roberts said, in his best Lugosi:

"Blood. The Coachman wants blood!"

We were all in on it, making all kinds of crazy noises and howling. We grabbed Clayton, who was laughing, and we pushed him, yelling all the time: "Blood! The Coachman wants to take a bath! The Coachman wants to take a bath!"

That was the last time I ever saw Clayton laugh.

"We got another pretty for you, Coachman!"

"Come and get it! Bath's ready!"

And we pushed Clayton into the hole, into that depression, holding him down.

"Another pretty, Mister Coachman!"

And Roberts started yelling: "Noch eine Schöne! Noch eine Schöne! Come on, Coachman, she's a beauty!"

Clayton started fighting us, which added to the fun. He was kicking, bucking, like he was almost crazy. Then we all heard, clearly, a voice from the dark, saying, very calmly:

"Fein."

We stopped. We looked around and Harry said: "What the hell?"

We listened, but there was nothing. And then Roberts said: "Fein!", and at that we were laughing again, and started to get up.

Clayton shook us off, and I noticed that he seemed really angry. He cussed at us, and we turned sheepish at once, as drunks will.

"Oh, come on, Clayton!"

"Come here, have a drink!"

"Clayton?"

He staggered away from us, and he began to brush the front of his clothes with both hands. He wouldn't stand still, and I started to realize that he wasn't angry. He was terrified. He had a look on his face like a man you read about, whose hair just goes white overnight.

Harry and Roberts turned nasty. They thought he was taking offense at nothing, and they resented it.

"Fine, then, go to hell, Clayton!"

"Yeah, who the –"

(—hell—)

"—hell needs you. Fine!"

(Fein?)

"Come on, Harry!"

Clayton kept pacing, but he looked unsteady, and he still kept up that brushing with both hands. I went over to him.

"Clayton. Come on, buddy."

He looked at me, but then his eyes were all over the moor, darting back and forth.

"Ellis," he said, "Ellis."

He was nothing like the crass, overbearing character I knew—and, truth be told, I had always feared to an extent. The change was sudden, and it had struck somewhere deep in his core, ferociously.

"Can we go home?" he asked, sounding like a small boy afraid of the dark.

"Sure, we're going. We're heading back right now," I said.

He shook his head.

"No. Not there. Can we really go home?"

All the time, he was brushing off his clothes.

He was shaking when we got him back to the cabin. Harry and Roberts were quiet now. We thought he may have been bitten by something, but there was no sign of it.

Eventually, Harry and Roberts fell asleep. I settled down to watch Clayton. He would drift off, lie quiet for a while. Then he would grind his teeth. Then his eyes flew open, but I could tell he was still sleeping, and they were sightless like a corpse's. It was as if his body, his eyes, responded to some alarm or danger. His eyes were looking for something, but there wasn't anything to see. They closed again, and he seemed quiet. Then he moaned, tossing and turning. I just kept watching him, half dead with fatigue myself, but shaken and riled up—too tired to get up but exploding with the need to move. I kept watching him, thanking God I couldn't see what was inside that tortured head.

Around four in the morning, his left hand started to brush the front of his clothes, gently.

When the sun came up, I felt better, realizing, with an odd sense of surprise, that the night had been completely ordinary aside from Clayton's tortured sleep. The lake, when the light hit it, was just as beautiful as ever.

Clayton, too, improved as the morning went on. We all went for a swim and had breakfast. And while nobody said very much, the day passed in wonderful normalcy. We played cards and talked about school. About eleven at night we went to sleep.

Forty minutes later, my eyes flew open as I heard Clayton moan. A frightened little sound. (Small as little...)

Then he sat bolt upright with a startled gasp.

"Clayton!" I called, and I turned on a light. He looked at me. He was drenched in sweat. He was breathing heavily, through his mouth.

"Are you all right?" I asked.

He looked at me, trying to place me. He ran a hand through his hair and shook his head.

The next morning, I took charge. I told Harry and Robert to stay at the cabin while I took Clayton into the city. We would find an apothecary, get him something to make him sleep, and not dream. He looked terrible—aged and sick. The walk itself could only do him good. So would getting away from the moor. I didn't want him to get up at night and see the lights dancing in the distance. I thought something terrible would happen if he saw the lights.

We set off, and I was pleased to see that he grew calmer with every step we took. He hadn't said a word the entire morning, but as our surroundings changed, he seemed to gain his composure to the point where I blamed myself for having waited a day before getting him off the moor.

Clayton began to tell me about the things he had dreamed in the night. The worst of it, he said, was the dream of something black and shapeless.

It was the size of a large bull, and it came towards him. It came at incredible speed, and in spite of its lack of any definite shape, he had a sense of it straining, running, in some way, with utmost urgency. Clayton knew it would take some time to reach him. It had very, very far to go.

But it was coming. Just as quickly as it could.

The heart of Klagenfurt is the elongated city square referred to as the "Old Square." It marks the extent of the town in its infancy. Today, shops inhabit the old buildings, which are beautifully restored, the facades painted and sporting flower boxes. In the summer, there is a constant, pleasant stream of tourists. The square goes on for about a mile, and you can't see one end of it from the other, because there is a slight curve to it.

I'm told that there is far more room in the old structures than any business has any use for. Not refurbished, these parts stand empty, and there are many passageways and silent rooms with doors seemingly built for dwarves.

At the very end of the square stands the old town castle, its courtyard open to the square. Painted a friendly white, it is featured on most postcards for sale in the city. This courtyard is where, over five hundred years ago, the Coachman met his end.

Clayton and I entered the square from the opposite end. It was a beautiful day, and I loved seeing the people. Shops, souvenirs, ice cream—at that moment, I knew I didn't want to return to the moor. I felt an intense revulsion toward that place, and the thought of the nights I had spent there filled me with a sick, dirty feeling. But here I saw tourists—pretty girls, children, and grandparents. I loved seeing all that life, and I turned to Clayton in the hope of seeing him similarly restored by the sight.

His face was rigid and had lost all color.

His eyes were wide open. He looked as if he had felt a tremor and was taking a moment to decide between a truck passing by and an earthquake.

"What?" I asked.

He stopped, blinking fast several times.

"Did you see it?" he asked.

"See what?"

He shook his head. He looked like he was about to say something, but he stopped himself and wiped his eyes. Then he jerked his head to his right.

"There!" he called, "Did you see it?"

"What?" I asked, increasingly desperate. "What am I looking for?"

He remained very still, and whatever had struck him seemed to be passing.

"It's nothing, now," he said. "For a moment, I thought everything was gray. For a moment there wasn't any color. Or hardly any. And the houses were different."

I shook my head.

"Maybe a cloud passed before the sun?" I suggested.

He nodded, and we walked on.

I felt a wind in my face for a moment that was uncomfortably cold and deeply unpleasant. It smelled of the moor.

My eyes sought out the tourists, as if for comfort. The storefronts were re-splendent in color—summer reds and bright greens and yellows. I glanced at Clayton, but I didn't want to ask him what he had seen. I turned back towards the Japanese couple I had noticed in passing. They were gone.

There was nothing where I had seen them but a moment earlier. I noticed the house, the store from which they had emerged. Its lines seemed blurry. I blinked, but it still seemed uncertain, as if seen through a shield of searing heat. The house was slate gray, and looked rough, like raw stone.

I inhaled sharply, seized by an urgent sense of danger.

Then I saw the tourists again. They were there, right where they should have been. The house behind them was a clothing store, painted green and white, colors playing in the windows. But for a moment, none of it had been there. They and the house had, I realized, just come back.

I stopped.

My breath was racing.

"You too?" Clayton asked.

"Just now . . ."

"Like the color wasn't —"

"And the people weren't there."

Clayton nodded.

We stood in the middle of the square. Clayton looked back in the direction from which we had come.

"We have to keep going," he said. He sounded urgent, and I wasn't sure why.

We passed the tourist couple. I kept my eyes on them, but nothing happened. Only when I turned my head forward again did I notice the building behind them.

No color. The lines were blurry.

I turned to face it. Now, two houses were rough and cold and empty.

"Jesus," I said.

We kept moving, and now I noticed it everywhere. The friendly facades seemed to blink in and out whenever I wasn't looking. It was like the dark, hostile stones were projected over them, coming and going, the old pulsing over the new.

I noticed a change in sound, too. At times, it grew quiet—very few voices. Then I heard a burst of French or English, but it faded away, crowded out like the stores and people. Two layers, the dark one gaining.

Fewer and fewer people seemed to be around, and suddenly I noticed one of the dark gray houses to my left. The lines were solid now, and whatever store had been there when we entered the square was gone. In the second story window was a dwarf. He wore a hat with a long, red feather in it. He leaned out of the window, staring at me, frowning. Then he spat down from his perch and slammed the heavy, wooden shutters.

I looked down and the pavement had changed. Hard-packed dirt, covered with straw.

"Jesus," I said.

And a man in a long, black gown caught my eye as he drifted past us and shook his head with a solemn expression. He put me in mind, of all things, of a plague doctor.

"Keep going," I heard Clayton's voice.

I felt it the moment he said it. Knew it was there.

"It's behind us, keep moving and don't look," Clayton said.

I wouldn't have turned around for anything. Whatever walked behind us was malevolent.

Plump, fearless rats stared at us from doorways and cracked walls. I heard music, six notes of a fast melody, repeated three or four times, then fading as quickly as it had begun. I had never heard that instrument before. It sounded like a moan, for all the gaiety of the tune. Who would dance to that?

We went on, the world becoming grayer around us, until we found ourselves at the far end of the square, standing in front of the old castle.

These weren't the white, pretty towers of the postcards. They stood iron-gray and harsh, with only a tremor about the very top of the towers, where their transformation was just finishing.

"Ellis," Clayton said, "It's here. It's here now."

It was so cold, suddenly, and so quiet.

I caught sight of what had come.

He stood in an archway of the castle, in the shadows. He wore an old, shabby tunic, and he had sturdy, bowed legs like a man who lives with horses. He looked at us from the distance, with palpable, cruel meanness. What had come was sick and filthy, and I couldn't stand looking at it.

"Damned boy...," Clayton said.

"Please," I said, "Please don't speak to it."

A bolt of light shot across the courtyard. The light had flashed off the ax blade.

"Our Father . . .," Clayton said, but he was stuck there, with nowhere to go.

"Our Father . . . our Father . . ."

The apparition moved.

It came in a queer, loping gait that carried it toward us at unnatural speed, as if it were pulled along, covering ten yards with every step.

"Our Father . . . our Father . . .," Clayton sobbed.

I couldn't stand it. I turned and bolted. I ran, knowing this devil's thing was somewhere behind me, that thing that glided at us from the archway. I ran, and I'm not ashamed, because I knew then, and I know now, it was Clayton it wanted, and there was nothing in the world that could have saved him.

I ran, seeing nothing, and a sound came from behind me—a howl, and a high, triumphant squeal—I was blind then, and I sobbed as I ran down that horrible, empty square. I ran until I saw a flash of red. Color! Then another, and I heard voices, and I saw more color, and I slowed, my eyes drinking it in, dying for it. And, finally, I found myself standing in front of that clothing store.

I turned around, and I saw one of the gray stone buildings fade away. It simply retreated, and I had the thought that there was some intelligence pulling the new over the old like a cover.

I sank to my knees on the pavement, touching it, crying, looking up every few moments expecting blurry lines again, expecting—

I felt the sun on my face, and the world was back and I was saying "Thank you, thank you!" over and over.

I stayed there on the ground until I heard screams from the far end of the square and, eventually, the sirens.

*   *   *

The Coachman

5 pm

Wilson fell back in his chair.

He looked around, wildly, coming to, feeling the room had just come back, was, perhaps, just regaining its colors.

Gwenna Luna stood by the window, looking out. It was still daylight. His desk lamp was on. He remembered switching it on.

The girl, by the window, looked like a sentry. She was, he felt, guarding him.

"How long was I . . .," he said.

"Not long," she answered, "It doesn't take long to dream." Then, full of excitement: "You saw it, didn't you?"

Wilson remembered every part of it.

"Pieces small as little mice . . .," he said softly.

Her face broke into a wide smile of relief.

"You saw it," she said, "I've never shown it to anybody. I didn't know if I could do it. But you saw it, you were there, you were . . ."

She was a child again.

Just once, I want—

I have a plan . . .

I want to say to myself—

"How did you do make me imagine it?" Wilson asked.

He had not expected this.

Hypnosis. Suggestion.

He had read of patients projecting their psychosis, dragging you in.

He had not expected her to be that good.

"You did see . . . the moor?" she asked, reading his face.

"It was convincing," Wilson said. "You have a talent."

"You think it's a trick."

"Not a trick," Wilson said. "A very powerful suggestion. A very, very powerful feat of mental suggestion. Well, a kind of trick."

She seemed crestfallen.

Wilson wiped his hand across his face.

(He had been on that moor.)

He thought, quickly, of what to do next.

She had turned back to the window. Clearly, his reaction had made her retreat.

Between whatever she feared and her disappointment, Wilson thought he was losing her.

He had been taken by surprise, had never encountered such strong suggestion, such vivid projection.

(He had been on that moor.)

He realized he had to get her back. He had to see again what it was she did. He'd be ready, this time.

"Don't give up so quickly," he said. It was a careful, calculated taunt.

She turned back to him.

"You said you found this man?"

She nodded.

He could see that her purpose was returning.

"Tell me something," he said. "What are you looking for out that window? What's outside?"

He had her back and he would be ready, this time.

She moved quickly from the window to his desk, crouching down next to him. "Lots of things can come to a window. Lots of things can come," she whispered.

"All right," Wilson said. "You show me."

She reached for the notebook and turned a page.

There were, again, those curious drawings.

Wilson stared at them.

He looked back at her, trying to catch her at it. But the book drew him, he could see movement there, on the page, from the corner of his eye.

The vague shapes on the paper formed a window and before it there was something large and dark, bending down. Bending down to see in.

My God, Wilson thought.

"There was a man lost in a fog and he met a friend," Gwenna Luna said. "We both wrote down the story, he his memory, I my dream. They were the same."

He was aware of her movement as he stared at the pictures. She was returning to the window.

She guarded him like an animal guarding a kill from another.

Falling. Falling.

What other animal?

A kill . . .

"Lots of things can come to a window..."

GROLLBEIN

I met Charles Windolph again by chance, and only because of the fog. Before that night, I had a polite acquaintance with him, the type you share as expatriates with a common language in a strange land.

I'm an American. He was an Englishman. That's good enough for drinks and an occasional dinner if you're far from home. I had met his wife and his son. But the night I drove across the pass in a fog I hadn't seen him for at least six months.

The night was awful. I'd had business across the border, and it was late when I reached the Austrian frontier on my return. Mine was the only car making the crossing, and a silent border guard waved me on. A neon-lit shop stood in front of cragged peaks that loomed behind it like storm clouds. The shop was bright, but there was nobody inside. I felt like the last living person who would see it before it would have to go through a long and unquiet night, when things could come down from those mountains. Then I drove into a tunnel and felt that leaving the border guard behind like that was unconscionable. Night thoughts. One gets tired.

When I emerged from the tunnel onto the narrow, winding road leading down from the pass into the valley, I hit the fog. At once, I slowed to a crawl and lowered the beams of my car. It was bad. One more damn thing before home and bed. At first, I could still see the looming pine forest to the side of the road, but gradually I was lost in a wall of white. I had to feel my way down that mountain, every sharp turn of the serpentine road a surprise. I had driven the route before, of course, but something happens in a fog. There's an old superstition I heard about once in Devonshire, of spirits of the forest leading travelers astray in weather like this. They watch people walk in circles from the trees and laugh. It's called being "pixie-led."

Elvis was on the radio. I turned it up, but the station faded and there was only a soft noise, erasing this century, making me feel alone. The next turn surprised me, and I almost overcompensated and drove into the abyss. Pixie-led. By now my car was barely moving. I remembered an inn along the road. I had passed it many times—an old house built of massive stone. My head hurt, the turns were getting harder for me to hit and I wasn't getting anywhere in a hurry. They were bound to have something hot. I could get some dinner. Maybe the fog would lift. At last, I saw the inn's light, an indistinct blur of orange behind a screen of mist. I turned off the road and into the parking lot. The pixies sat in the trees, laughing.

I couldn't tell you how many cars were in the parking lot any more than I could tell you what's under a blanket of snow. All was white around me, and I walked towards the orange light. The smell of the woods was strong and unpleasantly wet. I didn't like this walk at all. I felt vulnerable. I still wasn't over how Elvis had faded away and the silence that had followed him. The silence still persisted. There wasn't a bird or a rustle in the brush. There was just the fog, and my steps sounded heavy and ominous as I descended the wooden stairs that led to the heavy door. A face came out of the mist as I approached the door. I recognized the advertisement for an Italian beer brand—Birra Morretti. The old man with his glass of beer looked happy enough, and I was cheered at once. The poster was of this century, my century. We were all still here. I opened the door smiling, feeling that I'd made it.

Inside, it was dark and warm. A young woman behind the bar greeted me.

"Are you serving food?" I asked her.

"Yes," she said. "Sit down."

She disappeared to the kitchen, and I sat down and looked around the almost empty room. Then I saw Charles Windolph. I wasn't sure it was he, at first, not because he had changed in any noticeable way, but because meeting him here was too strange. We were at least an hour from the city we both called temporarily home, and to find an acquaintance as the only other guest in a dark, fog-bound inn is the kind of thing that doesn't feel coincidental. He sat in a corner, looking straight ahead. He looked tense and he wasn't eating. There was a cup in front of him, but it was empty and looked like it had been there a while. His hand rested on a small, black leather bag, the kind an old-time doctor would have carried on house calls. After a few moments I decided I'd better say hello. But I didn't like the way he was sitting there, not at all, not from the first. I had to remind myself of what I called him—we weren't friends, but at a stage of acquaintance that was still awkward away from our usual surroundings.

"Charles? Is it you?"

"Oh, hello, Henry," he said, quietly. He didn't seem surprised. I remember thinking that he looked like a man quite beyond any kind of surprise. I wanted to ask what brought him here, but checked myself, not wanting to be indiscreet. The idea of Charles Windolph harboring secrets was absurd; he was such a correct man. But you never know, do you? So right there I had run out of conversation. Charles saved me.

"Sit with me a while, won't you?" he said.

Oddly, I felt reluctant to cross the room and join him at his table. I didn't know what was going on over there, but it had the feeling of a death watch. I wanted no part of it. But I couldn't come up with any reasons justifying that aversion, and so I went to him.

The girl brought a menu and I ordered. Precious moments of normalcy, prescribed conversation. Then I was left with Charles again.

"What are you doing here?" I asked.

He looked at me for a moment with tired eyes.

"I'm waiting," he said. "Do you know today is the day before my son's sixth birthday?"

There was some sort of breakdown in progress here. Was his marriage failing?

"That's nice," I said. "How is he? How's your wife?"

"Well. Well, I hope," he answered, like one who hasn't had news from a hurricane-stricken island.

"My wife's fine, too," I tried. "We should get together again sometime."

"I've left them at the Monastery Maria zum Heiligen Kreuze," Charles said, so softly I could barely hear him. "Just for the night. They are well."

What do you say to that?

The girl came back with my soup then and saved me for the second time. A strong wind had started up outside, and I could hear a groan in the old building. I ate in silence. Charles' hand was still on the black bag. Was he mad? Had he done some violence to his family and gone on the run? He didn't seem out of his mind. He was calm, if tired. He was waiting; he had told me that much.

"Who are you waiting for, Charles?" I asked.

A gust of wind battered against the door. A dish broke with a crash, somewhere in the kitchen. Charles didn't flinch.

"Did you know that I had a family before? When I was very young."

"I didn't," I said.

"I had a wife and a little boy. They came with me when I moved to this country. Twenty-five years ago. Such a long time."

I wished I had gone on in the fog. This sounded like a confession, and a confession from a man you don't know well isn't a pleasure.

"They died, Henry," Charles said. "They were killed."

We sat in silence for a long time. Then Charles took his hand off the black bag, reached for my drink and downed it. He did this deliberately, and I sensed a determination about him. I had never seen a man so calm. Talking to me seemed to dispel the tiredness, and more and more of a purpose revealed itself.

"My boy was killed the night before his birthday," Charles continued. "He would have turned five. After it happened, I tried to remember everything about him. Everything he ever did and said, what made him happy. During the last three months of his life, for example, he had begun to speak of a friend, a giant."

Charles smiled.

"The giant came to his window at night and spoke to him through the glass. He was twelve feet tall. He had big teeth. His name was Grollbein."

"Kids," I said.

"Grollbein," Charles repeated.

The girl stepped to the window and looked outside. With a sigh, she turned away again and disappeared in the back.

"My boy told me the giant would come back to visit him on his birthday," Charles said. "And that, this time, he had promised to come inside."

The girl came back, and without asking she sat a bottle of brandy on the table. I nodded at her, gratefully. Charles had taken my drink and I wanted it.

"I was away the night before his birthday," Charles said. "When I came home, something had happened. They were both dead. The police said they were cut or torn to pieces. I never saw so many policemen looking haunted. They never caught the madman who did it."

"I'm sorry," I said. "I'm sorry, Charles."

"It was a long time ago," he said.

Something was strange about his story. If it was the night of his son's birthday now, his living son, why spend it away from his family? Why leave them at a monastery? Was Charles a superstitious man? Was it a sort of atonement for him to sit here alone in this desolate place?

"I was young, then," Charles said, "So it didn't destroy me. I concentrated all my efforts on my work. I worked until my energies were spent, and I could fall asleep at night. For years, I lived like that, a closed-off man. I made some money. I just went on, step by step. I didn't expect anything else from life after the tragedy. Simply to live decently."

"But then you met— " I ventured.

"Myra, yes," he said. "I never expected it."

He smiled when he thought of her. It was nice to see that. There was a lot of warmth in it.

"She's everything," he said, softly. "She really is."

His hand moved to his breast pocket, touched something there without him being aware of it. I wondered what he carried there, close to his heart. It must have been her picture, but I never found out.

"So, I took a chance," he said. "I started to live again the day I met Myra. We went places. We spent hours talking to each other, talking of fears and hopes and what a place the world could be. I took a chance and I never regretted it. I was so hungry for it, after all those years. Oh, it's been a wonderful life."

There it was again, the note of something ending. Of something having ended.

"When my boy was born, it was like I was complete again. You've met Brian."

"Yes," I said. "Sweet kid."

"He cried once, because he felt sorry for the little lobsters we saw in a restaurant, in a tank. You forget that when you're not around children. Feeling sorry for things," Charles said.

I hadn't felt sorry for anything in a long time. I guess he was right. But I wasn't lying about the boy being sweet. The result of a late love, he had all the happiness and gentleness of someone grateful to be born against all odds.

"I picked him up from school, oh, about three weeks ago," Charles said. "And he told me all about this essay he had written, about the time we went to the zoo— he's a good writer, you know, like his mother. He told me how the teacher had read it aloud in class, and I told him I looked forward to it, that he'd have to give me a reading when we got home. And then he said, out of the blue, without a moment's adjustment, he said that it'd been hard to write, because the giant kept talking to him through the window."

He took a drink, calmly.

"He said the giant's name was Grollbein."

I felt uneasy now. I'd have to walk out again after all, into the mist, and find my car. I'd be in the dark, unable to see a foot ahead of me. I didn't want to hear any more about his children, living or dead.

"That's quite a thing," I said. Charles ignored me.

"I mean, two kids making up the same name?"

He gave me a look that showed he knew I didn't believe that.

"Did you ever tell him, maybe? Or Myra?" I asked.

"I didn't. And Myra doesn't know about the giant."

"Is it from a book?"

"He's five. I know what he reads."

"Maybe at school?"

"I spoke to his teacher. No."

I knew there was an explanation. But it wouldn't come to me. So, I asked the logical question: "What did you do?"

"I tried to find out more from the boy," Charles said. "He told me that the giant had first appeared in a dream. They were in a garden together and the giant had picked the apples from the highest branches and given them to Brian. Then he had promised to visit very soon."

"Did he?"

"After a few days, yes. Apparently, he had come from the woods behind our house one night and looked in the window. Brian went to him because he carried a sheep with him and Brian wanted to see it."

"A sheep?"

"Carried it quite as easily as we would a cat, apparently."

"What did he say?"

"He asked if Brian had any brothers and sisters. How much he weighed. Brian mostly remembered the sheep."

"What did he look like?"

"Twelve feet tall. Big teeth. Brian said his face looked a little like the wild boar we had seen at the zoo. With a huge beard and eyes that were a pretty color."

"What color?"

"Red," Charles said.

I poured myself another brandy.

"What did you do?" I asked again.

"I asked Brian if he would do something for me. I asked him to ask the giant something from me. I wanted him to ask the giant to leave. To go away. Tell him he got one, to leave the other. Then I waited. By then I found it hard to sleep. I was aware of Brian's birthday coming closer. And I remembered."

"Did Brian do it? Did he ask the giant?"

"Yes, he did," Charles said.

"And?" I asked.

"He was playing, humming to himself. I walked into his room and asked him if his friend had been at the window again. "Yes, daddy," he says. "Did you ask him what I wanted you to?" I said. "Sure, daddy." He moved a little truck and made engine noises. "What did the giant say?" I prodded him. "He said you should mind your own fucking business," he said."

I got up and walked to the bar. I wanted to think for a moment. I had a hard time with the fact that I was listening to a story about a giant named Grollbein. That Charles Windolph was in some sort of trouble was clear. What to do about it was a different question. I'd have felt like a heel leaving him here, even if the day outside had been sunny and warm and the road open. Yet, my mind was telling me to leave, was screaming at me to leave and stop listening to the story. Then there was another gust of wind, rattling the door, and I realized I'd been standing at the bar with no good reason. So, I went back and sat down again next to Charles.

He took up his story as if I'd never left.

"One more thing about the giant that night," he said, "He didn't have his sheep with him. Brian asked about it, of course. Where's your sheep? No answer. Is your sheep coming back? To which the giant shook his head. And smacked his lips."

He laughed softly.

"Who are you waiting for, Charles?" I asked.

He turned to me with piercing eyes.

"You think I'm insane. It doesn't matter. But it will not happen again. Do you understand? Not this time."

He believed it. He believed that Grollbein was out there, roaming the woods, invading children's dreams, creeping up to their windows and asking them their weight, smacking his lips.

"What did you do next?" I asked.

"Next I procured a bottle of holy water from a church. I gave it to Brian. I told him that the giant wasn't a friendly giant. I told him what had happened to the sheep. When he comes back, I said, if he makes any move to open the window, you throw the water in his face. And then you run."

I was distracted by a low rumble outside. It sounded like nothing I'd ever heard. Something was moving.

"Two nights later, I was awoken at midnight," Charles continued. "I heard a roar that sounded like a wounded bear, I heard a loud crash, and then Brian came running into the room, yelling: "I did it! I did it!""

"Did you see anything?" I asked.

"I rushed outside. There was something. Yes, I saw something, for a moment. A shadow, huge, close to the woods. I think it turned towards me, because I saw a flash of red eyes. I saw the trees shake. I yelled at it, whatever it was. Told it to see me, the day before my boy's birthday. To come see me at the old inn in the woods. I'd be there, minding my own fucking business."

"You said that?" I was beginning to see Charles Windolph in a whole new light. There was another sound outside. A low rumble, closer this time. "You said that?" I repeated. What the hell was out there?

"The next day," Charles said, "my dog, a strong, good dog, was dead at the edge of the woods, turned inside out, torn limb from limb, every bone broken."

He took a drink.

"Grollbein," he said, "is angry."

"And tonight . . .," I began.

"Tonight is the night before my boy's birthday," Charles said.

He snapped open the black bag. There was a pistol and a box of shining bullets.

"I had them blessed by the abbot of Maria zum Heiligen Kreuze," he said. "Because a thing like that, that comes through dreams, is not of this world. That's where I left my boy and Myra, at the monastery."

"And Grollbein . . ."

"Grollbein is coming," he said, "Grollbein is coming."

We sat for a long time after that. There was a fear rising in me. I didn't know what I had heard outside in the woods. I tried to picture it, the thing coming out of the shadows, a sheep cradled in its arm, the eyes, the face of a boar. The dark voice whispering to the child, promising that the next time, he'd come inside.

"What happened to your first son?" I asked.

"Torn up like a rag doll," Charles said. "Torn up and eaten."

The lights flickered.

A dog barked outside, then stopped, abruptly. Cut off.

I wanted to be home. Had I lingered too long? I knew I couldn't face the fog now, not for anything. That walk to my car. What was out there? What had made that low, dark noise, that heavy sound? Was there a breath at the window? Was there a red eye peering in? Was I trapped?

And then there was a sound, unmistakable, unmercifully clear. It was a heavy tread outside.

I looked around me, desperate.

The steps came towards the door and something like a heavy chain was dragged across the ground for a moment.

Charles, calmly, took up his pistol.

The tread was on the steps now, coming down to the door. I looked to the crucifix that hung in a corner. It seemed to tremble.

Black, black fear. A child-eating giant. How much do you weigh? Is the sheep coming back? Tomorrow, tomorrow, I'll come in . . .

The door swung open.

The man was huge and swarthy, with dark eyes and a face like granite. He was smoking a cigarette. He nodded in our direction, then stomped towards the bar, steaming from the cold, and ordered a beer.

Charles didn't react. He simply slipped the pistol back into the bag.

I had to be elsewhere. I knew it. Far from being relieved by the appearance of the truck driver, he felt to me like the last man to board a doomed plane. I had a vision at this moment. I knew that the stage was set, I knew the gate was closing, the company complete. The people in this inn were lost. I wasn't one of them. I shouldn't be there. I knew. I knew that time was running out and that I had stumbled into a night I wasn't supposed to see. Run! Go! Time is running out! And beneath it all, the one thought, the one sentence: Grollbein is coming.

I jumped up from the table, fumbled with my coat. Charles didn't acknowledge me. I was like a ghost in this room: Charles, the driver and the girl—I was a ghost in this doomed place, I didn't belong.

"Grollbein is angry," Charles said.

I ran for the door.

"Life has been very, very good," Charles said, but he wasn't speaking to me anymore.

I ran up the stairs and into the fog. There was no way of knowing where my car was. But I ran. I knew I could end up in the woods. I could end up circling the woods, hearing screams and noise and shots. Then silence, as I fumbled sobbing among the trees, running in circles, then something heavy searching for me, looming behind the mist, reaching for me, red eyes. I knew I might end up in the woods, but I ran, I had to get away from the inn and the sense of death coming, death already there. I ran until I hit something, metal – a car, not mine, but a white one, metal. I was on the right track. Behind me in the woods, a tree cracked and a raven cawed, startled. I fumbled on, and there it was, my car. I tore at the door, and for a moment I was sure my keys were on the table in that inn. I was sure I'd have to flee into the fog like a madman, running for my life, losing my mind in a long scream. I closed my eyes and thrust my hand into my pocket, felt the keys, felt the keys, they were there, I had them – the door swung open and I started the engine . . .

Elvis came on full force, the radio turned up ridiculously high. I laughed, madly, then hit the gas and skidded towards the road, narrowly missing a corner of the stone building. I laughed, I felt so alive, so saved—I laughed, and then I saw it in the rear view mirror: A moment when the fog lifted into transparent swirls, when the orange light of the inn showed me a dark thing, a huge shape, vaguely human, bending over in its approach to the inn, bending like an oak tree falling to earth, reaching for the door with a long, muscled arm. I saw a flash of red, piggish eyes—and then there was a rumble, as of an earthquake, and the fog closed behind me, everything behind me was swallowed up, and I was alone with the dark wall of trees to my side, the haunted forest, and there was a shape by the side of the road that was a dog's dead mangled body, and the red, the red on the ground could be—and then the fog closed over that, too, and the road widened, and I was on the highway, and I went fast, too fast for this kind of weather, for this night, too fast, really, insane . . .

I slept late the next morning. Woke up in my soft bed, looking at the bookcases, the friendly bedroom lamp, the curtains. It was sunny. I smelled coffee from the kitchen, heard my wife singing.

Later, I read about the fire in the paper. The end of the inn, the death of my acquaintance Charles Windolph and the others. And whatever happened at that place after my mad flight, I know this: Nobody speaks about what they found, but there are rumors. Of huge bones, of a skull with horrible teeth. Of the pistol they found having been fired. And I know that Charles was a crack shot and that his boy is doing well. And this, too, I know: that I saw the boy, at his father's burial, that I found him in a side room afterwards and bent down to him with urgent secrecy and whispered the word "Grollbein" into his ear, and that he looked up at me, his eyes glowing with relief, and that he shook his head and whispered back to me: "No more . . ."

* * *

Opening his eyes, Wilson saw the window and thought, for a moment, that there was a dense fog outside. Then he saw the girl—still there, looking out—and he lost the fear, that terrible sense of having to flee, to find his car and leave that lonely inn before . . .

"There really was an inn there," Gwenna Luna said. "It burned down. And I told you what happened when I found the man. It was the same, what we wrote down. Exactly the same."

Wilson looked around his office, every detail a link to normalcy, to every day of fifteen years of practice. He seized on these details, brought himself back to his purpose.

He had, he decided, no way to tell how she was doing it. The question was: Why was she telling him this story? He could feel his mind reaching firm ground, could feel something like traction to his thoughts. Why this story, a story of a father sitting in an inn with a bag of holy bullets? There had to be a reason she brought him a story about . . .

"What happened to your father?" Wilson asked.

She was, he saw, taken by surprise.

"You haven't said anything about him."

She gnawed on her piercing.

If she had surprised him with her dreams, he was now surprising her with insight. Let's destroy the ancient fires, he told himself.

She looked at him with a quiet menace in her eyes. These were her old eyes again, the ones that seemed to have seen the crucifixion.

"He was a smart man," she said. "Like you."

"What happened to him?"

She waited so long he wasn't sure an answer was coming.

"He's dead," she said.

And nothing more.

Wilson leaned back, dissolving the tension.

"We'll get there," he said. "I can help you. I can help you if you work with me. Try to answer fully."

"When I said help," Gwenna Luna said, "I meant—"

"We'll get to the answers—why you carry all this."

"Answers?" she asked.

"Yes," Wilson said, "More answers, fewer mysteries for you, I think."

He smiled at her.

"When I said "help"," she said, "I meant something different."

"You probably did," Wilson said. "But this is how we do it."

She thought this over for a while. Then she opened the book again.

"We'll get there," she said, and he felt that she was building up her courage.

She turned a page.

"I had a dream all about answers."

Wilson glanced at the book and for a moment lost his breath because he saw himself there, in the drawings, sitting hunched over a desk. Then he realized it was a woman sitting there, and what had confused him was something they had in common: She was looking for answers.

Wilson was falling and the figures moved and he was afraid. Because the woman he had mistaken for himself was sitting at a desk and there was something behind her, crouching, and it laughed . . .

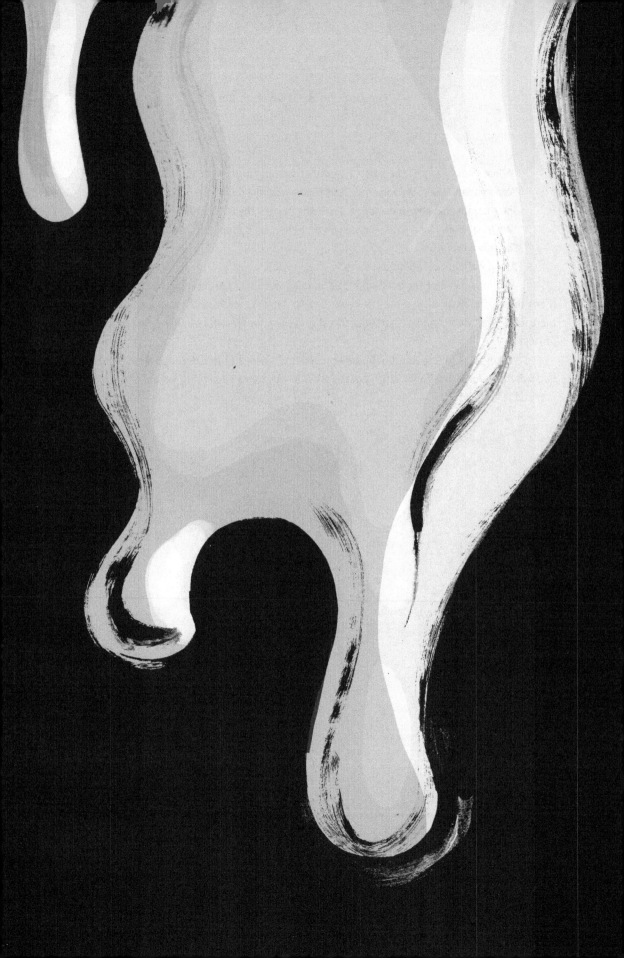

THE ARDALE GHOST

I was at Ardale University, working on my PhD in chemistry and doing some assistant teaching to pay for the privilege. I got to be friendly with one of the professors there, a chemist by the name of Gabriella Irwin.

She was blunt, fair, and renowned for not only having made students cry but, once, a careless dean. Top of her field, she was unassailable, but, I felt, impatient with academia at this point in her life. Her only true interest in those days was her notion of a certain kind of fast-drying paint—a revolutionary process she was hot on the trail of. She told me once about a dream she had, unusual for a scientist: to make a bundle and leave what she called the god-damned boy's club for life in the Swiss Alps. She had a greedy gleam in her eyes every time anyone mentioned paint. She spent every night working on her invention. The chemistry department's laboratory was at her disposal, and she had it to herself after ten o'clock.

Her trouble began in September, at the height of a late heat wave.

She sat in the lab and read and mixed and calculated, making, she told me, excellent progress. Until one night, when she noticed that she wasn't in the mellow, cheerful state that usually came on her when she worked. She felt, for no apparent reason, extremely uneasy. She said it was the closest she ever came to understanding the phrase about the hair on one's neck standing on end—an animalistic reaction, pure stone age instinct.

She noted the feeling, at first, with a scientist's detached interest and continued working. But after a while, she felt the overpowering urge to turn around and see if there was anything behind her. There wasn't.

A short time later, she told herself that it was late, that she had meant to finish work for the night anyway, and that she really needed some sleep before the next day's classes. It was all very true and sensible, but there was this nagging feeling on her walk home that she had been scared out of her laboratory.

There was one other thing, and it didn't improve her mood. Ardale University, from the days of its founding in the nineteenth century, had always had a tradition of a ghost. The ghost was supposed to be either the founder's terrifying wife or his oppressed and consumptive daughter. What all versions of the story agreed on was the ghost's nature. No mournful, wailing spook, this was said to be a violent and terrifyingly aggressive apparition, responsible, once upon a time, for a number of horrific but poorly documented deaths. Finding herself thinking, even in the remotest recesses of her mind, of this ghost cheerily depicted on mugs sold at the university bookstore was intolerable enough to Irwin's scientific nature to make her knock the heads off the flowers in front of her faculty residence as she passed.

The next morning, the fear felt like a strange dream. By the afternoon, it was almost forgotten. And when Irwin closed the door of the laboratory behind her that night for her next session of solitary research, her mind was all eager expectancy and fast-drying paint, with not a superstitious shadow hanging over it.

She had only been engrossed in her work for about an hour when, slowly, it came again: the same, overwhelming feeling of fear and hopelessness, what she described later as the cold sense of the grave. The impulse to run was almost unbearable. Irwin, however, made a concentrated effort to ignore it. She knew it was a meaningless warning, a product of overwork. And she wasn't a timid person. There was science before her on the desk, and science in every fiber of her body. She pushed on, doubling her efforts. Her pen flew across the paper, frantically. It was as if the pen fled in her stead, running and darting. She managed to become absorbed in her work again and when a particularly elusive notion started to crystallize in her mind, she smiled.

The smile was still on her face when she froze, having unmistakably caught a flash of something in the corner of her eye.

She turned.

There was nothing there.

But she knew it had not been her imagination. She had seen, for an instant, a gray shape of some sort. She sat for a while, listening to the silent building. The fan above her hummed steadily. Nothing happened. The beakers didn't throw themselves off the shelf. There was no moaning or clanking of chains. Yet she felt her heart beating and the unease that had plagued her was now a wave of utter, screaming fright.

She had seen something. Of that there was no doubt.

With a tremendous effort, Irwin bent over her desk again. Her pen was poised over the page. She kept shooting glances over her shoulder, catching nothing. But the moment the pen touched the paper, drawing the first line, there it was. Slowly, she turned, not wanting to warn off what she suddenly realized she already considered an entity. Her hand trembled. She saw it. A vague, gray shape that seemed to slowly grow and change. And with every sense she possessed protesting, shouting, warning, clamoring to run, showing repulsion and horror at what stood there, Irwin realized that the shape was developing form and that she saw, clearly, an arm and shoulder and legs, and that the thing behind her was slowly assuming the contours of a short, stout human.

At this, at last, her resolve collapsed, and Irwin jumped up with a frightened cry. She rushed from the laboratory and only stopped outside the chemistry building, where she paced up and down making small, startled noises and shivering at what she had been close to. The most frightening thing about the experience, she said later, was the certainty she felt of not only having seen what she had seen, but that the shape, human though its form appeared to become, had been extremely and aggressively predatory. That understanding had come to Irwin purely intuitively, and she was not to be dissuaded from it.

41

After half an hour's pacing, Irwin was calmer. Two hundred years ago, people would have fled from or prayed over such an apparition. Irwin was determined to find a cause for it. She suspected that there was something in the makeup of the laboratory, some physical peculiarity of its shape or furnishings, that had created the gray shape. If she had seen it, it could be investigated and dealt with. But apparently she was not sufficiently evolved from the simpler folk of two hundred years ago to have any intention of undertaking the investigation of the laboratory entirely by herself.

She didn't wake me when she called. I kept late hours. The way she put her request was: Would I mind helping her in the exploration of a somewhat startling phenomenon? Had to be that night. She sounded very calm. I had a notion of possibly being included in a paint-related breakthrough, a sort of "I want you" Graham Bell moment, possibly including stock options. So, I hurried to the chemistry building at once.

Any unease about the business Irwin might have had was certainly gone by the time I arrived. As she explained what she had seen there was a glow about her that I put down to the rush following an intense experience combined with an old, scientific bird dog getting a whiff of a fresh trail.

We went inside, and I have to admit that, after the story of a phantom materializing in the laboratory, the room felt invested with a certain powerful atmosphere. Seeing the abandoned petri dishes, the deserted desks and chairs, it did seem like they had seen secret things, and there was something ominous even about the regular, modern wall clock looking down on us with a blank, white face. A room where a ghost appeared is a haunted room, and that word becomes potent when married to a real place you stand in. A ghost story ennobles a place. "You know," I said, "that Ardale always had a tradition of a ghost."

"Don't," said Irwin, "be an idiot."

Then we solved the mystery.

We solved it by a combination of experiment and confirming research. The eerie feeling that Irwin had described, and that had preceded the manifestations, could be re-created quite easily. All we had to do was shut the door, place Irwin at her desk, and remain very still, as one would when engaged in work. If we waited long enough, Irwin claimed, in fact, to see the gray shadow again, though she never quite managed to wait long enough to see it take human form. But it did materialize, as before, behind her.

I didn't see it where I was then, by the door. But we did try the thing with me sitting at the desk and Irwin observing from across the room. And after a while . . . yes, after a while I did feel it. An overwhelming dread unlike anything I have felt before or after. I was shocked by it to the point of looking at Irwin in amazement, wondering how on earth she could have stood it by herself.

I was still marveling at this when, suddenly, I caught a glimpse of something small and gray behind me. I whirled around and there was a vague figure standing behind me, and I leapt from the chair and Irwin yelled: "Did you see her?"

It was this use of the word "her" that unnerved me above anything else. It took all of Irwin's powers of persuasion to make me stay. But in the end, I wanted to know. I wanted to know if there was an explanation.

We searched the place, analyzed all variables, changed positions, and so on, and very soon realized that the manifestations and the fear were strongest at Irwin's desk, with a few secondary spots of the laboratory producing similar, if weaker, occurrences. As to an actual cause, we soon centered our attention on the most conspicuous variable: It being a hot night, the large ceiling fan above Irwin's desk had been turned on during her nightly sessions. It was on now.

"An air current?" I suggested. But this seemed unsatisfactory and did not really explain what we both had seen. Suddenly Irwin smiled in a self-satisfied way.

"Of course," she said.

I felt like Dr. Watson, three steps behind the great mind. Irwin switched off the fan and made me sit at her desk. The difference was palpable. There was no feeling of oppression. The spook, I knew at once, had been exorcised.

"What did you mean by of course?" I demanded.

"It's gone, isn't it?" Irwin asked.

I agreed that it was, and she took the seat herself, smiling all the time. She leaned towards me, a generous magician about to reveal how it was done.

"Low frequency sound," she announced. "There's your answer."

She explained it at length: how certain appliances, such as, for instance, our ceiling fan, emitted sound with a frequency too low for the human ear to perceive, but there nonetheless. These sound waves could, as had been demonstrated experimentally, have an effect on the human senses, in some cases, if the sound was powerful enough, causing a vibration of the human eye. The pupil thus subtly stimulated will produce, as we confirmed the next day in the library, an unsettling and inexplicable feeling of unease in the subject. In certain cases, the vibration had been demonstrated to cause actual, convincing . . .

". . . visual hallucinations," Irwin concluded triumphantly. "I give you—your ghost!"

"Of course," I said. There it was.

"Shall I make her appear for you?" Irwin asked, putting on just a bit too much of a show for a professor of chemistry. She switched the fan on once more and gradually, as I kept very still, I felt it again, as terrible and strong as before. I got up from the desk before the vibration of my eyes would reproduce the gray visitor. I had no desire to see it again. We changed places and Irwin, delighted with herself, waited a while, and when the thing appeared cried out: "There she is! There she is!" with great gusto.

Then we tried it again without the fan, and all was quiet, the room just a room, the ghost laid to rest and the world a more sensible place. And when we went to the library the next day, we found confirmation of everything Irwin had deduced. We went away heroes to ourselves and much the wiser, I'm sure, about many of the haunted rooms and ghostly visitors that have their authenticity sworn to by hordes of witnesses who have seen things with their own eyes.

Except for one thing.

The next day being Sunday, Irwin didn't do any work in the laboratory. She did, however, go back that Monday night. By eight o'clock in the morning, she was dead. She was strangled by an intruder from behind as she sat at her desk, strangled with such violence that blood exploded into her eyes, turning them, wide and staring, an awful red.

When the police left, weeks later, I went back to the laboratory. Everything had been changed. Some pieces of furniture were gone. The fan, of course, was still there. I turned it on and sat where the desk would have been. Nothing at all happened. But of course, everything had been moved around.

There is an implication to all of it that has distressed me ever since. When we solved the mystery that night, turning on the fan, turning off the fan—if we weren't solving anything at all, then we were, clearly . . . toyed with. Watched and toyed with. By something that played along. Which implies intelligence, doesn't it? A certain humor, of a nasty sort, and conscious thought.

It implies so many things.

*　*　*

6:45 pm

Wilson's eyes opened.

"I see her . . .," he murmured, but at that moment the shape was already gone, faded into nothing, and the girl looked at him calmly.

Behind Gwenna Luna the window was a dark blue now. The daylight was going. Wilson found that this troubled him.

"It's getting dark," he said. And the girl nodded in a way that wasn't reassuring. She was, clearly, troubled by the idea of night as well.

So, she had warned him off answers. He thought of the gray shape standing by his side, the short, menacing figure.

"You don't want me too close to you," Wilson said. "I understand that." He resented the fear he remembered thinking of the gray shape.

"I'll get so close we'll find the source," Wilson said. "Don't you worry."

She looked away from him, almost as if losing patience.

Change direction, Wilson thought.

Get her back.

"I'll make you a deal," he said. "I'll accept your mystery. The dreams. What I can see in that book. Suggestion, some chemical on the pages, black arts or a miracle—I'll let that go. In return, you let me get closer. Answer my questions. About your childhood. Your parents."

Still, she was silent.

"Help," Wilson said, "isn't easy."

"But," she said. "we'll get there."

She sighed, suddenly a teenager again.

"All right," she said. "Ask me something."

"What's your earliest memory?" Wilson asked.

She thought about it.

"Being odd."

Then, with sudden resolution, she reached for the book and opened it again.

"There was a man, a dwarf," Gwenna Luna said. "Before he died, he wrote a diary. He was with a traveling circus. It cost five cents to stare at him."

There he was, hunched over in shadows.

"I dreamed every detail as he wrote it," Gwenna Luna said.

The dwarf was in shadows, writing, not eager to be seen. He had had his fill of being stared at.

Wilson looked up from the moving drawings, quickly, at Gwenna Luna.

"Being odd . . .," he said.

Then he was falling.

The dwarf was writing, furiously.

Something happened in that valley . . .

THE VALLEY
WITHOUT
LAUGHTER

You must understand, the dwarf wrote, that the vampire was my friend.

There was a tent, and in a small section of it, closed off by canvas walls, I would stand under a painted sign that identified me as Drollig Hansel. "Court jester to the kings of Europe, the only creature to have made the princess of Romania laugh after a long illness, a feat for which he was handsomely rewarded, receiving golden coins from her father's royal hand."

I stood under a bright light, which made it difficult for me to see anything. When a group of people was led into my section, I felt them as breath and shuffling feet, their presence more a sensed mass than individual faces. Eyes would sometimes gleam at me, flashes off spectacles. And when I felt their presence filling the tent, I began my performance. I was supposed to dance, to leap and caper. Clownish stuff. There was a secret cord that, when I pulled it, made my pants fall down for an instant and gave them a good view of my bow legs. The important thing was the laughter. There had to be laughter. There had to be laughter because of the other presence in the tent, unseen, but always there: Professor Nadoni himself.

He would secrete himself in a dark corner and watch. He watched all the acts, and sometimes, sometimes you could see, sticking out of the shadows, the long, thin form of his bullwhip.

He drank. And he was a violent man. We all knew the story of Billy Nolan, the poor boy with claws for hands, who had been so unfortunate as to push a child that had tormented him, somewhere in Illinois. Poor Billy Nolan had fallen in love with one of the girls from the trapeze act, and it had made it hard to take the insults. So, he pushed a little girl—a true monster, I'm told—and Professor Nadoni was out of his dark corner like a shot and dragged poor Billy away. He set the whip to work, and, well, the problem with Professor Nadoni was that, once he was good and drunk, he didn't know when to stop. He laid bare the boy's spine with that whip. You could see the bones shimmer in the gore, white as glazed china. They buried Billy Nolan the next morning and the girl, the girl from the trapeze, wept when he went into the ground wrapped in a bloody piece of canvas.

So, I made sure they laughed, that's all. I made sure of that.

I had one friend in those days. One friend in the world. His tent was set up at a little distance from ours. He wasn't considered part of the freaks. No. His was a different kind of act.

The Vampire.

You step away from the lights of the show, towards a black tent set up in the shadows. Enter if you dare. Pay your nickel and see the last descendant of Vlad Dracul, imprisoned by a secret charm, kept alive, fed on the blood of pigs. The charm's power might be waning, the moon might be full, and pig's blood not the thing the undead crave. But enter. You should be perfectly safe, I assure you. And you walk into the black, velvet tent, down a narrow passage. No music, no noise at all. You can hear your own breath. And down there, at the end, there it is, lit by flickering lanterns: A coffin. Standing upright.

Come closer. There he is, my friend. Tall, regal. As pale as any corpse. The lips drawn back so you can see dagger-like fangs. Nails long and sharpened. People would stand and stare in silence at him in his coffin. The stroke of genius was a small droplet of blood, fresh blood. You would notice it there, not at first, but in time, in the corner of his mouth, and it was so small and subtle that everyone who passed felt that it was their discovery alone, a thing not meant to be seen but accidentally revealed. And that made it horrible. And then, just when the crowd was entranced, mesmerized by the drop of red, his eyes would open. And you'd swear they were looking right at you, right into your soul. Oh, he was a fine vampire, my friend. It was showmanship of the highest order. I know he gave people dreams. They would take home with them the memory of those eyes. They got their nickel's worth of fear in that tent. Nobody ever laughed. I longed for it, you know. The darkness. The hushed fear. It was magnificent. You long for things like that when you spend your days dancing and dropping your pants so you won't be whipped.

Of course, he was a fake. But, in a sense, he wasn't. That's why he was as good as he was. He lived the part. His real name was Joshua Todt, he told me once. And he reveled in the closeness of that name to the German word for death.

He was a scholar. He traveled with the most extensive occult library, especially heavy on vampire lore, of course. He had a copy of the mad Frenchman Chabris' book On Vampyres, which was forbidden by the church two hundred years ago and destroyed wherever found. Wonderful stuff. He never went out into the sun, to maintain his pallor. His teeth were real, filed to dangerous fangs. His life had moved into the night long ago, and he would sit with me then, and we would talk and talk. Entire nights we spent in conversation. Speaking with him made the world large. He showed me that my own existence was a small thing, a limited thing, not a desperate eternity without relief but an episode. There was so much more. It was very good to hear that, to feel it. It was good to be his friend.

He told me that, when he lay in that coffin, when he looked at the pale faces surrounding him, and sensed that hush of fear, he felt a touch of it: the power of the vampire. To be eternal. And I know this about my friend: I know that he longed, with every fiber of his heart, to be real.

We came to the valley for the first time in late spring. The hill country. Things were different for us there. Profitable. But hard. It was an isolated place. Rich, clean, neat farms, settled since the 17th century. People of strong stock. A peaceful place of hard work. But I believe there is always an unfortunate effect in such prosperous isolation: a tendency toward cruelty to strangers.

This became apparent in our first show. I sensed it the moment the crowd filled my tent, filing in hidden behind the glare. There was a readiness to pounce. And when I danced, when I threw my hat in the air and did my cartwheels, I heard a little girl's voice saying, "I hate the little man," and then something hit me in the head, hard enough to draw blood. And they laughed.

Inbred little brutes . . .

We all noticed it. Things were thrown, acts were interrupted. Our drivers and riggers were drawn into fights in the local taverns, one of them beaten quite badly. But the oddest peculiarity of those people had to do with the Vampire act. Nobody went to it. The black tent stood, beckoning somberly. Yet, not a soul went inside. It had always been one of our most popular attractions. I had a strong feeling, watching people's faces as they contemplated the tent before hurrying off, that they actually feared for their health when they regarded the Vampire's lair. The air there seemed tainted to them. They were afraid that walking through those doors would do something to them.

I discussed this with my friend late at night. Come with me, he said, come for a walk. And even though leaving the show's campsite at night was a risky proposition, that night the Professor had passed out drunk in his wagon and we felt free to set out towards town. I often wondered what a picture we made as we wandered through the forest and across the meadows under the full moon that showed us the way. My friend, as always, wore his flowing black cape and seemed to be a part of the shadows. I must have looked like his familiar, my walk being so odd and jerky. Had we by chance met any of the cowards that dared not enter the black tent, the sight would probably have given them fits.

We left the woods and followed the dusty road until it turned into the town's main street, and all was silent around us. Lights were on in the houses, but not a soul was in the street, and a palpable sense of fear hung over the entire village in strange contrast to the arrogant aggression displayed by these people during daylight. We walked past the first few houses, and suddenly my friend stopped and pointed: "Look."

I saw it at once. At one of the windows, a cross was hung, and next to it, shimmering whitely, was a bunch of fresh garlic.

I understood. A death must have occurred, right before our arrival in the valley. A bad death. And the reason these people were not inclined to see a Vampire . . .

"Let's leave," whispered my friend, and of course he was right. We were in danger here. People in such fear catching us wandering about their village after a bad death could do things. Mobs have burned men for far less.

We spoke little on our way back to the camp. I thought of the people cowering in their beds, listening for noises, praying to be spared. And when the sun came up, they would set out for the show again, and some girl would yell that she hated the little man, and all of their fear and their anger at their own superstition would find release, and then a bottle would fly and blood would flow.

Any hope that we would leave that valley was dashed the following morning. Professor Nadoni awoke late and made an announcement. The show had made money during the time it had been here. There had been bloody noses, true, but there had also been money. And, as the Professor had found out, a week's wait would bring the annual spring festival, when hundreds of farmers from surrounding valleys would gather at the village.

We heard the rumors.
It was the town drunk who had died.
He was bled white.
And a child had disappeared.
Whispers and rumors.

The show must go on.

Professor Nadoni, in typical fashion, adjusted very quickly to the local audience we faced. If cruelty was what they craved, that had to be taken into account. Of course, not by protecting us, but rather by providing it himself. So, in the days leading up to the festival, he developed a new show, a new line-up of thrills and excitements for the people of the valley. For ten cents, you could now throw a pie at a freak, whose head protruded from a wooden board with a hole in it. Come on, throw it hard, they can take it. Freaks have hard heads. And if you feel like throwing anything else—a pebble, perhaps, or a tin can—well, who's to say anything about it, as long as you paid your dime first.

I, too, was demoted from Court Jester to the Kings. I closed my eyes and waited for the next hit, piecrust smeared over my face, blood trickling from my forehead. I looked over at poor old Anne, who was a gentle woman and a dwarf, who had up till now herded trained piglets in an act called "Lilliput Hogfarm." I blinked away the blood and looked over to her, and I saw that she was crying as she waited with her head stuck through a board, while one of the nasty farmer's children took very careful aim at her.

Then something happened.

I had just washed the blood off my face after my last stint as a target and I went to the back of the camp, where my friend's black tent was. I needed to talk to him, needed his counsel and sympathy, and, more than anything, his vision of a grand world of possibilities. I stopped when I saw the woman.

She was beautiful. Pale, a marble head with long black hair, above a slender frame hidden by a flowing cloak. She stood contemplating the black tent, and there was a smile on her face that was both wise and far away. Then, without seeming to move at all, she entered the tent—a glide it was, perfectly still and smooth—and I stood alone in the night in wonder.

I sat down to wait. She did not come out. The camp grew quiet, and still I was watching the black tent, and not a sound emerged. It stood in perfect stillness. A moment later I was aware of movement, of small things appearing below the tent flaps and disappearing into the high grass. Mice and roaches, they were, always present in camp, always hiding in the tents. They were running. As if what was in that tent was an abomination.

She came back. She came back every night, disappearing into the Vampire's tent and not emerging until an hour before dawn. Nobody seemed to notice her, except me. I noticed, because I wanted to see my friend but was prevented by this visitor. I craved his voice and his calm, and sleep was a stranger to me now, the way things were with the show. We were all three creatures of the night, the beautiful woman, my friend, and I. I felt connected to them in that way, and it comforted me. I did not begrudge her the time with my friend. I couldn't begrudge her anything. She was, in her cold and remote way, the most beautifully perfect woman I'd ever seen. I withstood my daily torment and kept my sanity because I knew I would see her at night, my one moment of beauty and stillness in all the madness. She was hypnotic. And I knew I would speak with my friend at last, and he would tell me everything he knew about her mystery, and we would all be connected, drawn together in a silent night that was all promise and silence and dignity.

It should have been a shock when, after an interval of several days, I at last saw my friend face to face again. It should have been a shock, because any physical transformation of a familiar face shocks. Death moving closer always does. But it wasn't shocking to me, no. I knew who she was. I had come to realize it, watching her. She was the bad death.

My friend was lying on a cot in the very depth of his black tent. His pallor had increased to the point of inhumanity. His face was a skull's face. He lay with his eyes closed, and I tiptoed to his side, and reached out, and slowly turned his head. And I saw. Two red marks on his neck—frayed, strangely dry holes. The signs of a slow death, a slow death that ends in unnatural life. My hand shook. What I had felt about the woman was now confirmed. Yes, such things could be. I was looking at them. I was looking at such things . . . And then, just as in his act, his eyes opened. They were weak now, nearly drained of life. For three nights his shadow had visited him, and there wasn't much left. He guessed my thoughts. He whispered: "One more night," and nodded. I kept my eyes on his wounds.

"One more night until what?" I asked, but I knew. And he knew I knew. He smiled at me, and I could see his fangs gleaming in the light. And I trembled.

"Oh, my friend," he said, with a fading voice, the voice of the grave. "My good friend. I'm happy."

And I backed away as he sank into a deep sleep, and before I left his tent, I took from the shelves the mad Frenchman's book about the undead, because I knew, right then, that there were things walking in this valley that were unnamable, and that I would have to make a decision soon about one thing: life or death.

I spent the rest of the night reading, jumping from page to page in the mad text, words of blood and prey and charms and warnings. Sentences burned themselves into my brain, so that I can still, years later, see them on the page, see them as they were before me that night. "Once infected, the prey of the undead becomes undead himself. It is a known fact that entire regions have, in this manner, been depopulated by an outbreak of vampirism." "There is no cure but death itself, and death is a mercy."

The festival, which would bring farmers from many miles distant, was a day away.

The next day was like a dream. Few farmers or children came to our tents, I suppose because the fair was about to begin and promised bigger thrills. So, there wasn't much abuse that day. Not that it would have mattered to me, for my mind was elsewhere. I had not slept the night before but read in Chabris' book until I saw the sun come up, dispelling for the moment the shadows and visions. And I had watched the black tent, and thought about the sunlight penetrating my friend's sanctum through a thousand little cracks and crevices, and of the pain the light must cause him, the nausea and revulsion. He was so close, now. He was hers, nearly hers. And I went about my day in a dream, not laughing, not dancing, but waiting for what would befall this valley, watching the laughter and the families holding each other, brave in the sunlight, not knowing what was here, what had arrived, what was about to be unleashed.

And when, in the evening, one of the riggers went to see my friend the Vampire and reported him missing, when speculation ran through the camp, and fear of the wrath of Nadoni, who raged and stomped about his circus, who, we knew, would find an innocent tonight to pay in blood for the desertion, when everyone was talking and cowering and speculating—I secreted myself under one of the wagons and I wept. For I knew what had happened, and so I cried for my friend and his longing, I cried for his deep voice saying, like a child, "I'm happy."

And when at last I emerged and went to my bed, I wore a golden crucifix around my neck, which I had made a vow not to remove as long as we were traveling through this haunted valley.

The first night of the fair, a desperate man was looking for his three children, whom he had sent on their way with a nickel apiece and instructions to have fun. A cry went up and down the valley—the dead town drunk was remembered, as was the child that had disappeared before we came. All of this I watched, sitting on the roof of a wagon, my legs dangling freely. I sat and watched the people, who knew so much less than I, and they shot glances at me in passing, saw a grotesque, hunch-backed thing, swinging its legs and watching, with some knowledge in his eyes they lacked, and they hurried on, remembering me as part of the horror of that night. I watched them running and organizing and talking and helping and searching, and all that came to my mind was: "Entire regions have in this manner been depopulated." And a second thought, following closely: "You don't know what's out there."

Drollig Hansel knows.

They found the children dead and bloodless in a ditch. That night, there hadn't been any slow, elegant feeding. That night, it had been fast and greedy, not to claim but to gorge. Not careful bloodletting, but famished butchery. I saw them carry away the three bodies. Don't cry, I thought. They'll walk again. Soon. Entire regions have in this manner been . . .

Again, I read. The entire night, the mad Frenchman's voice was my guide. Death of a vampire. How to kill. You burn the heart, of course. Separate the head from the body. Bury both facedown, the mouth stuffed with roses and garlic. Also, if burning is impractical, the heart may be pierced by a stake.

Why was I confident that I could find them? Because I knew my friend's mind, of course. In that entire valley, which cowered in fear and looked for answers and solutions, looked for comfort and knowledge, only I possessed it. Only the despised, abused, revolting dwarf could do anything about anything.

The show was closed—nobody came after these last deaths. Yet, Nadoni dared not leave, afraid that a hasty departure would be construed as guilt. We were all in danger now. Someone would pay. Nadoni was a brute, but he wasn't a fool. It would have been suicide to try and leave the valley now.

I slept that entire day and night, the book for my pillow, the cross around my neck. I slept because I knew what I had to do, and that I needed all my strength to do it. The heart must be burned. A stake driven through the chest. I slept all that day in the heat, through the worry and the guessing and the fear. I slept through the night, through the hunt and the prayers and the tears. I slept to be ready. I slept because I would be the one to undo my friend and his beautiful shadow.

I dreamed of madness, of dancing for the dead, of going on a knightly quest, of being spat upon before slaying a dragon.

The old church. We had passed it, my friend and I, on our way to the village that night. It had fallen into ruin long ago, walls crumbling, brush growing first over the paths, then the stones, at last climbing up the still-proud steeple. It had been built with ambitions of eternity, in stone and heavy timber. I had seen my friend notice it, and I knew that it fit his view of the world in its slow contemplation of never-ending things and patient decay. I knew with the utmost certainty that this is where he had gone now.

My preparations began at midnight. I rose from my bed and, touching the book one last time on my way out, I stepped into the cool night. It was dewy and fresh. Something called in the forest. The camp was quiet.

I had a hammer in my belt and now went around the back of the main tent, picking up the spare stakes left there in case a strong wind made it necessary to reinforce the tent's lines. The stakes were heavy and clanked ominously as I carried them in the crook of my arm. I could carry four of them and no more. That was fine. Four would be a good day's work, provided the number included the woman, who was the source of it. I set off for the village first, to find a church. There wasn't a soul abroad. Every house I passed had the shutters drawn. Once, a dog barked, but nobody came to investigate. At last, I reached a church and entered. I filled a flask with holy water from the font at the entrance. The font, that night, seemed to glow with a mysterious radiance, a power. The sacred space knew my errand. Following a sudden inspiration, I dipped my stakes into the water as well. This had not been mentioned in the book, but I felt it to be right. I was ready now. Confession had been advocated as a necessary part of the preparation, but I did not feel the need for it. I felt that I had done penance already, years of it. Confessing after penance was backwards.

I set out to the ruined church. The dark was just beginning to turn, the coming of light sensed rather than seen.

By now there were noises coming from some of the houses I passed. Cows were mooing from the stables, milking time. I heard doors closing, muffled voices. Then I was on the road again, out of the village, and on my way.

If I hadn't had my mind on the things I was about to do, if I hadn't been mentally investigating the ruined church, I would have seen them coming. But in a moment's inattention, the sort of inattention that can cost your life, I missed them in the gloom and only saw them when it was too late to leave the road. There were four of them. The oldest looked to be about fourteen, the youngest, ten. I supposed they were on their way to some early chore, or returning from some nightly mischief.

"Look," one of them said, "It's a freak."

Then they were silent as I approached, and I realized that I still had a chance. They were, I was sure, weighing effort against the fun to be had. The freak might just not be worth the trouble.

I nodded as I passed them, saying "Good morning," trying to get away on manners. They slowed, but they hadn't stopped yet. There was still a chance. I noticed one of them carrying a basket covered with a cloth. It was an errand, then. I hoped it was important.

I took a few more steps when I heard the voice behind me.

"Hey, freak!"

"Hey, stubby!"

Then something hit me on the head, cold and wet. I reached up and my hand came away yolky. Then another egg hit me, and I heard them laughing, and as I dropped the stakes and stood there being pelted, listening to them taunting me and laughing as they threw their eggs, I knew that I was lucky and they weren't out for blood and that, in a minute or so, they would let me run. Fortune was with me.

When they had gone laughing down the road, I picked my stakes up from the dust. I had lost time. There was a pale color to the world now. The church was close. I was sweating, and my muscles hurt from carrying the heavy stakes. I stumbled on down that road, and at last saw the ruined steeple, and then the walls. A bird called, then flew away, and there was utter silence in the forest, the silence that marks the line between night and day, the breath after the long nightmare. I saw, high up around the tower, several bats returning from the hunt and disappearing into the black eyes of the shutterless windows.

I concealed myself in the brush and peered out from the shadows, watching the entrance to the church, long since robbed of its doors and standing open like a scream.

Not a breeze or a rustle. Had I missed them? I was still certain of my guess; I knew that this was their lair. But had they returned while I was delayed on the road? Then I heard, far away, the crying of a child sounding terribly across the dark, silent forest. The sound came closer, desperate and lost. Then a dark growl, as of a wolf, and then the silence again, the terrible silence following a done deed.

Then I saw them, and I stuffed my hand into my mouth to keep from screaming.

They came from the shadows like mist, side by side, at a slow walk. My friend's mouth was smeared with blood, and his lady carried in her arms the limp and white body of the dead child. They reached the door, and for a moment, as they entered, their flowing elegance and regal, awful dignity, disappeared. They bent over as they entered the church, and with the blood and the corpse, and the animal shine in their eyes, with their bloodstained fangs, they were, for the moment, revealed as beasts, the red-eyed things they were, driven by appetite and blood lust. Their beauty, at that moment, was gone, and only the inhuman thing that animated them was visible, and it was that which almost made me lose my mind in a scream and run madly into the forest and flee this cursed spot.

Yet, I stayed. I had found them. I picked up my stakes, held them tight. And when the first ray of the morning sun broke through the trees, when the first bird began to sing, then more, then more, I rose from my watching place and approached the ruined church and went into the blackness.

Morning had not happened inside. The thick walls deadened all sound, and the air was stifling. I stood still and listened; there was a draft somewhere in the walls that sounded like a low whistle. Then a single ray of light began to travel across the wall, slowly. Then another. The sun was rising, gaining on the dark. I had the advantage now. I moved on, my steps sounding loud on the old flagstones. At the far end of the church, where the altar would have been, I saw steps leading down. I moved towards them. I was sweating freely now, cold sweat of fear, and my hair rose like an animal's, alert and sensing in all directions. I felt a surge of panic course through my body that shook me. But I didn't run. I stared down the stairs into the crypt. Was this a dream? I looked at the stakes in my hands—they had no reality. There was no explanation for them. I was mad. Nothing but the blackness below and the moaning whistle of the wind. And then, a creak. I turned my head. It came from a partially collapsed wall to my right. My hands shook at the sound, and I dropped a stake. Grabbed it at once and held it close.

Something was moving there.

Something was squirming like a worm in a small crevice of the wall. I stared at it, knowing that after seeing it, whatever it was, I would never be the same man.

It was white and small, and at last I realized I was looking at the dead child. It wiggled and twisted, so maggot-like in its pale repulsiveness that I gagged.

The dead thing tried to squirm further into the crevice, and I realized that it felt the ray of sunlight moving closer across the wall and was trying to get away. It made a gurgling hiss and at last disappeared in the shadows of the cracked wall, lodged in there tightly, and the last I saw of it was the teeth, opening and closing on themselves, reminding me of a blind leech plucked off a body and pumping its entire body into a frenzy looking for the lost feed. And then, at last, even the teeth disappeared into the dark, and I was alone again. So, the child was moving again, moving already. They spread quickly. How many in a week's time? That small thing would set out for prey once the sun was down. And whatever it found would hunt the night after that. The curse was moving through the valley.

I went down, into the crypt, remembering prayers I hadn't heard since the death of my mother. I went down, looking for the source.

The crypt was low. A normal person would not have been able to stand upright. The atmosphere was that of a coffin. No sound reached here. But there was light—a patch of warmth that came from the entrance I had used and formed a square of safety on the earthen floor. I stepped away from it and into the blackness. They would be in the furthest corner of the crypt. I felt for them, not with my eyes, but by instinct. I was a hunter now, sniffing them out. As I felt my way along the stone walls, feeling their rough surface under my hand, I heard a sound above me, and for a moment had the terrible feeling that the child-thing was crawling down into the crypt after me, teeth opening and closing, cutting off my retreat. But I pushed on, my sweat-slicked hands holding the stakes, holding them so my knuckles were white.

I could hear my own breath.

And there.

At the very end of the narrow crypt.

A tomb.

It was massive, hewn of stone.

The letters "MASON" were written on its side, in withered script, but I knew that whoever had been the owner of this burial place was no longer here. What slept there now had not been buried in a church, under an altar. It had crept in one night. And as if to confirm my thoughts, I stepped on a thing that cracked loudly under my foot and, looking down, beheld a pile of bones tossed carelessly onto the floor.

The heavy top of the tomb was ajar—a slight crack remained between the frame and the cover. And all the feeling of evil and doom that permeated the place came from that little hole. What lay in there wasn't dead. And I stared into the small opening until I thought I would go mad.

Then I inserted one of the heavy stakes and pulled on it like a lever, and with a loud, grating movement, the tomb slid open.

I stood gazing down at it.

At both of them.

They lay together, and they held each other.

My friend looked as if asleep, and I remembered his words to me: "I'm happy."

She was more beautiful than I could have imagined.

I looked at their hands, which were intertwined, and thought of my friend's long years of solitude and loneliness.

Happy.

I raised the stake and placed it against his chest.

It would be a release.

He wasn't alive any longer.

I was the only one. The only one to save this valley.

I raised the hammer, looking away from the hands intertwined.

Goodbye, old friend, I thought. Goodbye.

And a fly landed on my forehead and changed it all.

I don't know where it came from.

It must have followed me down into the dark.

It landed on my forehead, and, a reflex: I dropped the stake and swatted at it, and I touched my forehead as I did.

The fly disappeared.

My hand was sticky. I brought it down before my eyes, and it smelled of eggs.

I looked down upon the body of my friend and his lady.

I looked at my hand, and then, fearing my thoughts, I dropped to my knees and searched frantically for the lost stake.

I found it, and again it was pressed against my friend's chest, and I raised the hammer and I knew it came down to me, life and death, there was no one else, and yet, and yet . . .

"Entire regions have in this way been depopulated . . ."

I could save them.

And yet . . .

Evil things that crawled out of their holes at night and preyed upon . . .

And yet . . .

A new word, a chilling word . . .

Slowly, it crawled into my mind. Until it filled it utterly.

"Revenge."

I had never, ever, thought of it before.

My hands trembled.

Entire regions . . .

Revenge . . .

My hands shook. And slowly it dawned on me that I was smiling.

Thinking of them, in their beds.

I could save them all. There wasn't anyone else.

He was my friend.

"Miserable," I whispered.

Then louder.

"Miserable bastards."

I hadn't smiled in years.

And now I trembled with the power, I shook with the certainty of it, I remembered, I remembered the laughter, years of it, there wasn't anyone else, it was a new word, a new thought, I was so sure of it, my course, my deed, it was so certain now, so clear.

Death . . .

One year later, on our trip to the West, Professor Nadoni's Traveling Circus passed through that valley again. Yes, I still danced for a nickel, did cartwheels and all the rest. And, yes, Nadoni still drank and threatened. That didn't change, no, at least not yet. But the valley, oh, the valley had changed. We didn't stop there, this time. There was nowhere to stop. The village had disappeared. People had moved on. Trying to outrun some fear, I suppose, some fear they wouldn't speak about to outsiders. The fields were barren, reclaimed by what had always grown there. Houses stood open, and who passed by helped themselves to whatever was left of any value. For some reason, though, all who passed made sure they were gone before nightfall. The people of the region were silent about what it was they wished to avoid. We passed quickly, and nobody mentioned the events of the year before. It was the kind of place you passed in silence and with a feeling of dread. Yes, the valley had changed. There wasn't any laughter anymore, no laughter at all.

* * *

8:38 pm

Coming to, drawing himself up from the lingering sense of death the dwarf's dream had left him with, Wilson felt a physical toll from entering these people's minds or, in any case, Gwenna Luna's creation of them.

He was unnaturally hot, his breath came heavily, and he felt a reluctance to become fully conscious that suggested a fever.

Gwenna Luna watched him from a distance. The window behind her was black and the light entirely artificial.

The wind outside had picked up, and now and then a thin wail could be heard.

"Why don't you admit," the girl asked, "that you were there?"

There was a knock.

"Yes?" Wilson said.

Sadie stuck her head in the office.

"Would it be all right if I left now, Dr. Wilson?" she asked. "There's a storm, and I'm worried about the roads."

He looked at her for a while, the welcome ordinariness.

"Dr. Wilson?"

"Yes, of course."

She seemed to hover.

"I'll close up," he said.

"Okay."

"Good night."

"Good night!"

She shut the door.

He felt that her departure separated him one step further from everything he knew. But he also felt strengthened by the interruption. He still had a world behind him, a reality. He turned back to Gwenna Luna, who sat on the window sill, one leg tucked under her. She watched him steadily. She was waiting for his next move.

He thought of Sadie, driving, listening to the news, getting gas on her way home, he thought of billboards along the freeway.

(. . . you were there . . .)

He thought of billboards.

He thought of the haunted valley.

There was no difference in how he remembered them.

"Let's get back to what you were telling me," Wilson said.

Gwenna Luna tilted her head.

He looked at the cuts on her arm. Noticing, she shook down her sleeves.

"I know who you're afraid of," Wilson said. "The source of all this. Your mother, who filled your head with all this . . ."

He could barely see her face now. He adjusted the lamp. She looked, once the light fell on her, much like a girl again.

"Yes," she said.

"I'll show you that she was just a woman. Strange, frightening perhaps . . . but, when you take away the eyes of a child, just a woman. She can't hurt you now."

The more he talked the better he felt.

He picked up his pad, sat up straight in his chair.

"An ordinary woman," he said. "You said she disappeared years ago?"

She nodded.

Then she slid out of the light and into the shadows as she went closer to the book. She placed her hand on it.

"Sometimes," she said, "they come back."

"There's nothing she can . . ."

"Ask me another question," she said.

He stopped, unsure.

"Ask me about my father again," Gwenna Luna said.

She was a voice from the dark.

"What happened to your father?" Wilson asked.

"Mother killed him. People say she ate his heart. Then she disappeared."

She opened the book.

Those shapes, dreadfully familiar.

"Sometimes," she said, "they come back . . ."

The shapes and lines, the falling . . .

There was fear surrounding that little, mean man sitting in that shabby room full of old, bitter things. That old man in the pawnshop . . .

Wilson was falling.

Sometimes they come back . . .

A PAWNSHOP
NEAR
WHITECHAPEL

Two dogs gave the first sign that something was coming. Until that day, the day of the first snow, Tuttle had spent his waking hours uneventfully in the dusty shop and his nights in the small flat in the back.

Had spent his days seeing the desperate of London slink through the door, to the misleadingly happy chime of a little bell.

That same bell had accompanied the luckless into Tuttle's when it had been his father's, his grandfather's, and his great-grandfather's. For a hundred years, it had been the same bell, the same place, essentially the same Tuttle: a small man crouched behind the counter, with wild, unkempt hair and the clothes of an under-taker. There was money in people's misfortune. That was the premise of that shop. The present Tuttle was the product of generations of granite. Pity had been bred out of that family.

"Sold it this morning, madam."

The woman gasped.

Her husband's mother's brooch gone because of a delay of twenty-four hours. The good pieces sold fast. When she left, she was crying, and Tuttle took a bite of toast. A marionette, dangling from the ceiling like a hanged man, stared after the woman, grinning. The sound of the bell died away.

"Come again," Tuttle called after her.

It was time for the dogs.

Tuttle had a mutt named Wellington, a clever thing that had learned to open doors when only a puppy. Wellington, as was his custom, dozed in his corner near the door, and Tuttle watched him while finishing his breakfast.

Lately, whenever Tuttle had sold a piece and faced down a heartbroken customer with a worthless claim ticket, he had noticed Wellington raising his head and looking at him with an expression very much like reproof. Tuttle thought he had caught that look again just now. He eyed Wellington suspiciously. Then he shook his head and made a careful mark in his ledger book, where it said: "6453 - Emerald brooch."

That, he thought, was that. Hadn't been that good a piece. Small stones. Not worth all that fuss. Certainly not worth a dog's indignation.

"Was it, now, boy?" Tuttle said sourly.

The dog raised his head with such a violent jerk that Tuttle nearly dropped his fountain pen. ("To Father with Love" was engraved on it. Tuttle was childless.)

"What?" Tuttle exclaimed, but Wellington ignored him. The dog stared past the dusty violins and canes in the window out into the cold, clear winter's day. Tuttle sat very still, suddenly unable to move until the dog put down its head again and dozed on. The dog didn't.

Tuttle waited. Felt the tingling of the hair on his neck, secretive and ominous. Wellington got up, eyes fixed outside, and growled. Tuttle watched in fascination. Wellington was no longer young. He never exerted himself. This was unprecedented.

Wellington stood like a statue. Very slowly, the tail moved downwards. Very slowly, it disappeared between the animal's legs.

Tuttle, fountain pen still poised over the ledger book, waited a few more moments. Finally, he decided something had to happen.

"Down, boy," he said.

The effect was instantaneous.

Wellington leapt into the air, all four paws leaving the floor. He yelped and ran for the door. In a flash, he had it open and was gone.

Tuttle stared at the still-moving door, open-mouthed.

Then he noticed, where the dog had been an instant before, the puddle where Wellington, most fastidious of animals, had lost control.

As the light grew dim, Tuttle was still trying to make sense of it. He was by the door, wiping Wellington's mess off the floor, mumbling curses. In spite of the cold, Tuttle had left the door open after the dog's flight. Why had he run? He paused in his work, watched his heavy breath, then contemplated a patch of sunlight on the floor. By God, were the boards so old and faded? He never noticed—there had never been a patch of light like that in his shop. Such brightness. Perhaps it wouldn't have hurt the place, Tuttle thought, unreasonably. Perhaps some brightness like that, now and again, would have made his dog stay. He sniffed the air and smelled snow coming. He couldn't take his eyes from the light, but suddenly it lost its brilliance and faded before his eyes like a rapidly wilting flower.

Tuttle turned and looked outside.

There was snow coming, coming fast. The cold sun had disappeared, and the light was strangely blue and dark, the shapes of the facades across the street standing out as if drawn in heavy ink. Then came the first flake, then another. The sky was heavy and gray. Softly, it began to snow.

"Oh, my," Tuttle said.

There was no one in the street. Tourists never ventured down his seedy side street. He saw only one living thing: A dog. Not Wellington. This one had just entered the street, coming from Whitechapel. It trotted in the direction of his shop through the swirling flakes.

Tuttle didn't like that dog. Even from a distance, it looked the size of a small horse. It was black, muscled, masterless, and mean. It moved with—Tuttle couldn't find the word—something unusual for a dog. Reason. Purpose. In his head, Tuttle heard Wellington's yelp of fear. He pulled the door towards him, only leaving it open a crack, holding it before him like a shield. The black dog came along the other side of the street. It trotted on, its tongue hanging out, and Tuttle could hear heavy breaths, like bellows working. He also heard a clicking of paws on the pavement, a clicking so loud the animal had to have monstrous claws.

When the dog arrived opposite Tuttle's pawnshop, it stopped.

Tuttle pulled the door shut just a little more.

The black dog looked at him.

Still the sound of bellows.

Monstrous claws.

The black dog looked straight at him. It looked like it was smiling. Not a friendly smile. Then it went on, down the street, click, click, click. The snow thickened, swallowed it up.

Tuttle shut the door. He was uneasy. Had to have his eyes checked. For he could have sworn that, before moving on, the black dog had given him a wink.

Snow kept falling throughout the afternoon. It was nearly dark outside, and no lamps had yet been switched on. Tuttle sat behind the counter, and his shop had never looked so gloomy to him. He missed Wellington. The damned mutt. He touched the radiator and found it satisfactorily hot. Suddenly, he longed for a fire. Friendly light. He looked up at a soft, creaking noise. The marionette that hung from the ceiling. (The man who had pawned it, looking heartbroken—grandfather carved it. You heard all stories in this business.) The marionette that hung from the ceiling slowly turned in an unfelt breeze, until its eyes rested on Tuttle. A grinning hanged man. Tuttle shuddered. There had to be a draft.

He was uneasy in his own shop. The shop of his father, his grandfather, his great-grand . . .

There wouldn't be any customers today. The streets wouldn't be cleared for some time, and the cars passing sounded muffled. Snow kept falling, almost as quick as rain now. Better to bar the door, Tuttle thought. Better to lock and bar that door. He shivered. Uneasy in his own shop, fancy that. He didn't know why, couldn't explain it. Didn't know that the thing the dogs had given warning of was reaching for the doorknob.

The bell rang.

All he saw, at first, in the dim light, was something black moving into the shop like a mist. Then a streetlight flickered to life, and the blackness formed itself into the shape of a short, thin man. He wore a cape and top hat, its brim covered in snow. The last echo of the bell faded, leaving an utter stillness, the only moving thing the silent snow, looking orange as it floated to earth past the light of the street lamps.

Tuttle felt the cold.

"The door, please!"

The intruder stood looking about him. He was in no hurry, seemed like a traveler studying fascinating ruins.

"The door," Tuttle insisted. He was always firm with customers. Let them know who it was that needed money.

The man made no motion for some time, then shoved the door shut with a bang. A porcelain doll dropped a teacup, which rolled across the counter. As soon as the door was closed, Tuttle felt an extreme aversion against being alone with that man. He heard, in his head, his own voice, calling for his dog, his own voice, pitiful and frightened.

The man slid up to the counter. He looked up to Tuttle, and the weak light that illuminated the ledger showed his face. He was pale, but behind his eyes Tuttle saw pure heat. A thin sheen of sweat glistened on the face, as if there were a bonfire going on inside. In his expression, there was something perpetually amused.

"Tuttle, " he said, and his teeth were like fangs.

Then he winked. Tuttle thought of the black dog. There wasn't a sound from the street, soft silence.

Oh, Tuttle thought, to be in the country. A nice country fire.

"You'd be," the dark man said, pausing, "the grandson, I'd wager."

He laughed. It wasn't a good sound, and Tuttle hoped it would stop.

"I've come for my things."

The man was too young to have known Tuttle's grandfather. For all his color of a corpse, the man was no older than thirty-five.

"Your things?" Tuttle asked.

The man produced from his pocket a claim ticket. Tuttle took it, and it almost crumbled to dust in his hand. The ticket showed number forty. The number was written by hand, not like the printed tickets Tuttle used now.

"This is—rather old," Tuttle said.

"I've been away," said the dark man.

"The item may have been sold."

"I hope it hasn't," said the man.

They faced each other across the counter.

"I better have a look," Tuttle said.

"I hope it hasn't," said the man.

He found it in the farthest corner of his shop. It sat on top of a cabinet, a burlap sack with a ticket attached to it. Tuttle could read the neatly written number 40 from across the room. In all his years in the shop, the sack had never caught his eye. Had just been sitting there, waiting. Tuttle brushed off the dust, gently. When he lifted the sack, there was a metallic clink from inside.

It had been on top of the cabinet, uncrowded. As if every other item in the shop had kept its distance, horrified.

The man opened the sack as soon as it was handed to him. Tuttle leaned closer to see.

The blades shone like new. Small blades, fine precision instruments. Long blades, thin and quick. A heavy one, serrated, a butcher's tool heavy enough to cut bone. Tuttle caught a whiff of something—thought it was gin, and sweat, and sex and fear. It didn't make sense, and it was gone in a moment.

"Now," said the man. "You'll be wanting your money."

Tuttle glanced at his ledger. Neat rows of check marks.

"That's all right, I think," he said. "All right."

"I tell you what, boss" the man said. "I'm a bit short just now. You let me have my things. I'll be back tomorrow with your money."

"Really," Tuttle said, "There's no need."

"I'll come back tomorrow. I haven't a base in London at present."

A base? Tuttle thought. A base?

His visitor turned and walked to the door, the sack under his arm.

When he reached the door, Tuttle called out: "What's your name?"

The thing mumbled: "Jack."

Tuttle couldn't sleep.

What to do?

For the first time in his life, he wished for a friend, someone to ring, who would help him puzzle out this matter, and who would be in the shop with him tomorrow, so he wouldn't have to face that second meeting alone. Jack.

Well, there were no friends. Even Wellington was gone. Tuttle had always prided himself on his cunning. He had the ability to gain the upper hand before people knew they were in a contest. His mind would be all the friend he needed.

Tuttle settled down with a concoction of hot chocolate and rum and pulled a blanket over his shoulders. In his rooms, he had a fireplace, and he lit it in spite of the radiator. Every once in a while, he peeked outside past the curtains, and every time it was still snowing. A lonely track crossed the street, the footprints rapidly filling in. Where was everybody? At home, watching nothing on TV.

What did he have to go on? The claim ticket, of course. Number 40. And that mention of his grandfather. Tuttle smiled at his own skill as a detective.

"I'll know soon enough, Jack," he said aloud.

A crash came from the shop, and Tuttle leaped from his chair. He was frozen for a moment, then rushed to the door connecting his flat to the shop and opened it. The shade of a ceiling lamp—a cheap thing—had fallen, not for the first time. Watching it roll across the floor, Tuttle felt his heart pounding.

"I'll know soon enough," he thought, "Jack."

But he didn't say it aloud this time.

About an hour or two before dawn, Tuttle found what he was looking for. Number 40 appeared in November of 1888. Tuttle followed the entries in his grandfather's ledger, followed his grandfather's harsh, clean writing. His grandfather stared from every photographic portrait with a force to make the glass in the frame crack. Tuttle followed the old man through June, July, through watches and musical instruments and pistols and candlesticks. Followed 29 to 30, 33, 35, August, September, October.

The entries were neat and cold, sold items marked with the same merciless mark he used himself, a Tuttle trait. Only one moment of emotion crept into the entries of the old man, when, next to a mark denoting a trumpet, he had written:

"Killed himself when sold. The fool."

Entry number 36 (cufflinks) brought the ledger into November of 1888. 39 was the last on that page. Tuttle moistened his fingers on his lips. They came away dry. He tried again, but there wasn't any spit.

Don't turn the page, he thought.

Jack's there.

Tuttle pulled his blanket tight.

Here goes.

Number 40.

"Knives."

He could still read that word. He could still read that word, even though the entire line between 39 and 41 had been crossed out in black ink, crossed out with a force that would surely have broken the pen. The contrast to the clean, unemotional lettering of the previous entries was like a slap in the face. This uncontrolled scrawl—Tuttle gasped at it. What had done it? He thought of his grandfather's granite eyes. What had done it?

Next to this desperate attempt at deletion, something else was written:

"Thurs: Mary Kelly, NOT HUMAN—God"

Scrawl. Fear. Animal fear.

You couldn't live near Whitechapel all your life and not know the name of Mary Kelly. The name of the last one. The one left gutted on her own bed, looking barely human (NOT HUMAN), left in a heap, on her own bed, by Jack the Ripper.

At last, Tuttle went to bed.

He drifted off as the first cold light came through the curtains and a moment later he was dreaming. The vision consisted of nothing but his dog, running down a country lane, without looking back. Frothing at the mouth, coat drenched in sweat. Nothing but that image. And his grandfather: Screaming loudly enough to crack glass.

Tuttle hid the old ledger book, cleared away the blanket and cup that had kept him company. He dressed, made breakfast, sat on his stool behind the counter. But he did not unlock the door of his shop.

Who was that man? Who was out there with Jack the Ripper's knives?

Tuttle had no idea what to do next. He sat, pretending to enjoy his toast. Waited.

His eyes found the radio sitting on the counter.

He turned it on, just when the newsreader said: ". . . murder in Whitechapel. A woman's body was discovered this morning and . . ."

In his mind, Tuttle heard the voice of a movie newsboy:

"Read all about it! Read all about it!"

A woman had been butchered.

Left in an alley.

Tuttle sat behind the counter. Thinking of the gleam of those knives, the stench coming from the old sack. That big knife that looked almost like a saw. The woman had been a prostitute. A trail of red on the snow, widening, had led a policeman to what was left.

Run, Tuttle. Run.

The bell rang, and Tuttle leapt from his chair.

Jack stood in the locked shop, a black shape against the window.

"You're nervous, boss," he said.

He came closer.

Tuttle looked into that face. Remembered what had frightened him about it.

"I had to get started," Jack said. "My, London's still a busy place, isn't it?"

"What do you want with me?" Tuttle managed.

Jack reached into his pocket. He dropped some money on the counter.

"Your fee. The loan," he said. "Now it's settled."

The bills had dark stains on them.

Good God.

"Who are you?" Tuttle asked.

A hideous grin.

"I knew your grandfather."

"You better leave here," Tuttle said, "I won't tell."

"You asked a question of Saucy Jack," he said, "You'll have an answer."

"No," Tuttle squeaked.

"Who do you think I am?"

Tuttle shook his head.

Jack leaned close, which was unbearable.

"I'm not some lunatic who merely thinks he's me," he said. "You see, I like ripping, and ripping's what I'll do."

Tuttle shook his head.

"Here's what you do, boss," Jack went on. "Look at that book, by that man John Thomson. The book with all the pictures. Look for the pub. That's what you do, there's a nice clue for you."

When Jack straightened up again, there was a faint clink of knives.

"Now," he said, "What'll you give for that?"

He tossed a ring on the counter, and as Tuttle watched the cheap, feminine thing roll across to him, he knew that simply having it in his possession could get him arrested.

"Don't run, boss," Jack said. "I'd find you. And I only rip whores, but who knows what I'd have to do if you ran out on me like some cunt."

Tuttle's hands were still shaking hours later, between the stacks of the library. His hands were shaking so badly he could hardly turn the pages. A clue.

He had found the book without difficulty—John Thomson's photographs were published in a volume that combined them with Henry Mayhew's accounts of London chimney sweeps, rat catchers, beggars, and dancing girls. Characters indeed. Tuttle turned page after page of hard street faces: Italian street musician, 1877. Drunkard, 1880.

Look for the pub, Jack had said. There's a nice clue.

Old seaman, 1878.

Boy with—

The pub.

Tuttle leaned over the book.

They were lined up in front of the Whitechapel pub, some smiling, some holding up pints of beer. They stood in the alley, the proprietor in the center, some of the patrons linking arms and toasting each other, squinting into the sun. 1888. That was the year, wasn't it? By November, Mary Kelly, the last, would lie on her bed not human.

Tuttle found him on the right.

Nobody toasted Jack, who wore a cape and top hat and smiled. Smiled at Tuttle from an image taken in 1888.

The second victim was found three days later.

Her mutilated torso lay in the gutter, her head was neatly set upon a wall. Two policemen, it was reported, had been sick at the scene.

Tuttle noticed his hair falling out in great clumps. He looked across the room to Jack, who sat in an antique chair (old widow, rent money due) and attempted to cool himself with a gaily colored Japanese fan (Tuttle had forgotten its origin).

"Oh," Jack said, "The fun we have."

He made quite free with Tuttle's pawnshop by now, spending hours there, sometimes talking, sometimes looking through the old things like a man reliving scenes from childhood. No one ever entered the shop during those times. Once, Tuttle had seen a desperate looking woman reach for the door, but she had turned away with a look of repulsion and fled.

"A fine city, still," Jack said. "You ought to enjoy it more, boss. You'll be sorry, believe me, later on, for everything you've missed. Come along with me sometime, why don't you? I'll show you a time."

I'm at heart a country man, Tuttle thought. Why haven't I been out of the city in years? (A little brightness every now and again, and the dog would've stayed.)

"I hate the snow," Jack said, because it had begun to fall again. He turned to Tuttle.

"You know what happened to me?" he asked.

"If you wish to tell me—" Tuttle said quickly. He had to hit precisely the right measure of deference. He had learned. It was crucial if one wanted to stay away from any talk of ripping.

"You do or you don't?"

"Yes, I do," Tuttle said. "No one has ever puzzled it out, to my knowledge." He's vain, he thought. Why else write letters to the press?

The Ripper laughed.

"They thought I was a doctor. Ha, I say. Had to be a surgeon, right? I tell you, any reasonably handy fellow that fancies a bit of a woman's liver will find a way to get at it neatly. That's what I say."

Tuttle felt his gorge rise. He hadn't eaten in days, not since Jack had begun to tell stories, sitting in that damned chair.

"Had me drowned in the Thames, hanged for some wife-killing in Dundee, locked up in an asylum. They thought I was Prince bloody Albert Victor, for God's sakes."

"None of this is true?" Tuttle knew a certain measure of interest had to be shown. Jack was starved for human response. Wherever he had been, he hadn't gotten it.

"No," he said, "Not true."

The Ripper leaned back and closed his eyes.

"Christ, she's a joker, isn't she?"

"Who?"

"Fate," said the Ripper.

"After that Kelly woman, I was off English whores. Police went through my room one night when I was out, that was a sign, wasn't it? So off I go—to America. In New York I did two, but nobody much cared there, and they was the same tarts as in London, but then there was a fine one in Buffalo. She just kept livin' that one, for the longest time . . ."

Help, Tuttle thought.

"It was a Chinatown girl they almost buckled me for. Damn it, that was a near one—shot at, I was, with a pistol. Had a light right in my face, they did."

Tuttle raised his head.

"What about the girl?"

Jack looked at him for some time. Bitterly.

"Lived," he said.

Tuttle found a grateful smile flash across his face and he touched the corners of his mouth, in surprise. The news about that girl made him so grateful he could have cried.

"So, here's what I'm thinking—what does a man do when he gets into any kind of a spot in New York? He goes West, that's what. I never ripped any girls from the West, and I'm thinking of their voices, all kinds of sweet sounds, just waiting for me, and I feel pretty good, then, I don't mind telling you. They got Bowie knives out West—you ever seen a Bowie knife? So, I get on a train, with the last of my money. And this is December, now, you must remember, and we're about to cross the mountains, and they have some mountains, they do—and the higher we go, the thicker the snow flies, till there's nothing but white out the window."

Tuttle saw a huge, black train spouting steam and, through a window, the Ripper's face, leering into the gloom, hungry, in his bag a knife the length of an arm.

"We stuck in that snow. Avalanche or some devil's thing, and the train stops, so close to the summit you can almost see it."

Jack was sweating now—the heat he carried inside seemed to get stronger. The unholy fire flared up, and looking at that face, you knew that inside this creature there were screams.

"I made a little mistake, then," he said softly.

He looked at Tuttle as if admitting to a great wrong.

"I've been called impulsive, you know."

He seemed to expect disagreement, and Tuttle quickly raised an eyebrow and blew air through his nose, which seemed to do it.

"We're almost at the pass—so I want to push on. And this man tells me, like he knows, that an hour's walk will do it. There's a station at the summit, he says, you'll be fine, but he stays where he is, with that train, you know the type, so I set off alone, and I walk and I walk and, nature being the bitch that she is, there comes a fog, and now I don't know where I'm going, it's white everywhere, and there's voices, and I hear a whistle—Whitechapel police, and a dog's barking —and I'm walking in circles, I knows it, but I can't do nothing about it, and I hear coaches, and voices, just like back in London, except I'm on this mountaintop in the middle of America, where there isn't anybody for miles, and I hear this voice sayin' "There he is, I tell you, that's the one we been talking about"—and this, too, sounds like an Englishman, and I keep walking, until I come to in the snow, and I'm all snug, not cold at all, and I wait for sleep and I lie there, not remembering lying down, and snow's falling, and I'm thinking: What an end. All fluffy."

Was that what became of Jack the Ripper?

But there was more.

There were three shapes.

"Three shapes," Jack said. "I open my eyes, and there they are, walking out of that white like they can smell me. And they're real enough, after all those voices and things, they're real—looking at me, me looking back at them, half frozen as I am. Three mountain men they were, bundled up in furs, big fellows, all painted up in the face. And hungry they looked, too, hungry they looked, no doubt about that."

He played with the fan, opening and closing it. He was agitated. Suddenly, he flung the colorful thing away.

"They helped me up, nice and easy. Ah, Jack, you're a made man now, I say to myself, not your time, yet. I'm thinking of a big fire, something hot to drink, a few of them furs. And those three grin at me as they pull me from the snow, they smile at me, and I think to myself, wherever they take me, maybe they got some women."

Jack, for the first time, didn't look at Tuttle, didn't look at anything but that fire inside himself.

"Starving, they were. That's why they were so happy to see me. They cut me up and roasted me and ate me up, and they broke my bones and sucked out the marrow."

He rose from his chair and put on his cape and hat. The knives jingled eagerly.

"Don't wait up," he told Tuttle. "I'll be late tonight."

"Where—" Tuttle started, and the Ripper turned back.

"Where were you . . . after? All those years?"

The Ripper looked angry now. Tonight was going to be bad. Mary Kelly bad.

"Fucked, I was. All those years."

Then the smile returned. He came back, close, and leaned in so Tuttle could smell the cloud of death on the thing's clothes. Tuttle gagged, covered his mouth with his hand.

"Then," the Ripper said, "Saucy Jack escaped. And don't think that's ever been done before. So why don't you try and run, why don't you try and squeal? Oh, you better not."

He was not back by morning.

Tuttle was alone until the woman came in.

The bell jingled, and Tuttle noticed the baby she was carrying. The child looked malnourished. The woman—the closer she came, the more of a girl she revealed herself to be—looked like she had been crying. They both were dressed too lightly for the cold, and her nose was red.

"Good morning," she said politely.

Tuttle nodded.

When the child was carried past the antique chair, it let out a scream as if pricked by a needle. The girl shushed the child, looking embarrassed.

The girl held out her hand. The two pearls were exquisite, the settings perfect. Tuttle saw them right away for what they were. Two hundred years old if they were a day. A little brightness now and again, and maybe the dog . . .

"What'll you give, please?" she asked. "They're old, my mother said, nearly a hundred years. I think they're real, are they?"

He knew she would take whatever sum he would offer. One look at that baby's hungry eyes told him that. He had experience. Oh, God, did he have experience. Re-sell those in a day. No chance she'd be back for them. They were the last, hidden treasure.

Tuttle put the money on the counter.

It was more than she had expected. It was more than she had dreamed of. It was far more than the pearls were worth.

She smiled, but already there were tears. She tried to hand him her treasure. He put his hands behind his back. She looked confused. Then she looked suspicious, because she was a pretty girl.

"One moment," Tuttle snapped. He suddenly felt desperate. He rushed to the flat and returned with two bottles of milk.

She looked at him in wonder.

"You're lucky today," Tuttle said, "Now go and don't speak of this to anyone, won't you?"

She shook her head.

Tuttle pointed at the pearls.

"These are magnificent," he said. "Very valuable. Any museum would pay you handsomely. Don't be cheated. There has to be an auction. That, or keep them. Because you're lucky, and there'll be better times." He felt a tingling on his scalp, a giddiness that left him short of breath. This felt like flying.

She looked at him for a moment, then suddenly kissed the air, turned, flushing, and rushed from the shop.

I'll be a better Tuttle, he resolved. And he almost cried, because he was so afraid.

The dreams, that night, were horrible. As he turned off the light, Tuttle had the secret hope of deep sleep, perhaps, he was embarrassed to admit, as a sort of reward for the girl. Instead, what came was this:

A goat-headed thing crept close, and he smelled its foul breath.

"Where is he?" it hissed. (You can't smell anything in a dream, he told himself. Then gagged at the stench.)

"Where is he?"

"Catch me when you can."

A woman laughed.

"Do you have any idea what you're fucking with?"

"You'll say anything but your prayers."

A woman laughed.

"Oh, no," she suddenly said. "Oh, please, murder!"

The goat-headed thing turned to the huge black dog.

"This is bad. He's here someplace," it said. The dog nodded and walked away, claws clicking.

"We'll see you later," the goat-thing told Tuttle. "Right?"

Slashing knife.

Oh my—

G—

Oh my God

God— what— my—

He was up, standing next to his bed.

Morning, soaked in sweat.

Oh, God. What visions.

Dressed, not feeling better, Tuttle went from the flat to the shop.

I wanted to be a better Tuttle, he thought. He tried to conjure up that woman's face, the baby, like a charm.

My God, what dreams.

The door to the little storeroom flew open.

The Ripper emerged. He was without his hat and in his shirt sleeves.

"Morning, boss," he said.

"You—" Tuttle said. Something dawned on him. The dreams.

"You were here all night?"

Jack grinned. He rapped his knuckles against the wall.

"Just a thin wall away," he said.

Those dreams.

"You look—" Tuttle said. Then he was stuck.

"Sated," he finally finished.

Jack flung himself into his chair. His sleeves were rolled up. His forearms had a reddish look, like after a thorough scrubbing.

"You look sated," Tuttle whispered.

He saw it ooze from under the storeroom door. Saw the blood ooze out from under that door.

"I so like having time," the Ripper said.

Tuttle's knees buckled. Those dreams.

Just a thin wall away.

There wasn't a woman.

There was blood on the floor, on the walls, all four walls, on the ceiling.

Frantically, Tuttle cleaned, scrubbed, boiled water, scraped, soaped, feeling himself, with every trace he removed, sinking deeper and deeper into the filth and muck that was Jack.

Then he noticed the door. Tuttle stopped. There was a small, red handprint on the door, fingers splayed. ("Oh, please, murder!") He stared at this last, pitiful trace of the vanished woman, the small, red shadow of her right hand, low, close to the floor. He stared at it, and wept, and wept, shoulders heaving, and then he wiped it off and felt like an animal.

The church door flew open with a bang that lost itself in echoes, growing increasingly insignificant in the calm, cavernous sanctum.

Tuttle looked around wildly. He dipped his hand in holy water, surprised to find it painless after what he had done. Flesh melting down to bone, that would have been just, that would have been—

He stumbled towards one of the side altars, towards a statue of the Virgin. She looked calm and blessed. She looked like she would hear him, care about the thing under his roof, the blackness and the guilt. She'd want that thing stopped, care about what that hell hound did, care about that bloody hand print on the door. With shaking hands, Tuttle lit a candle. Then another. There were rows and rows of them, ranged all along the altar unlit, waiting to be thrown into spiritual battle. Tuttle lit them all. There were more on the next altar. He went for them. He lit candles frantically, racing through the quiet church. There were more Saints, faces stern or gentle, a blur to him—they held keys, swords, books—he lit and lit and lit.

When a priest entered, carrying fresh cut flowers, the church was blazing with lights that flickered excitedly in the draft, signaling an urgent message. Tuttle looked up from his work and found the priest watching him. He couldn't speak. Couldn't speak of this enormity.

"Pray!" was all he managed to yell out, before he turned and fled. Tuttle rushed from the church, leaving behind him a puzzled priest and a golden, flickering cry for help.

Never before had Tuttle noticed so many poor people in London. It appeared he met them all on his way back to the shop, and their eyes haunted him. Christmas decorations blinked frantically in all the shops. A wall was pocked with snow, where little boys had been practicing their aim.

Better Tuttle. Better Tuttle.

Tuttle lost his footing in the snow and nearly fell.

Saw, when he closed his eyes, the hand, red, the small hand.

Alone in the shop.

Had he dreamed it?

A man brought in his grandfather's saber. Tuttle gave a fair sum. When he quoted a rate of interest, the man's face lit up.

"Awfully generous terms, aren't they?" he asked.

"It's only money," Tuttle said. "And times are hard."

Wherever it was that Wellington had run to, it was sure to be a beautiful place.

Exhausted, Tuttle sank into sleep by evening, his head on the counter, the door to his shop still unlocked. When he came to, everything was dark, the door half-open and the room bitterly cold and full of shadows. Inside the door stood the black shape of Jack the Ripper. Watching him.

"Havin' a lie-down, boss?" he asked.

All these candles lit against this thing.

"There's whores out, Tuttle," the Ripper said.

"Is there nothing," Tuttle said weakly, "that can stop you?"

The shape didn't move. Tuttle watched the snowflakes behind it, falling softly. Inside that blackness, he could feel that smile coming at him and he turned his eyes away, just for a moment, a moment of not looking.

"No," the Ripper said.

A car passed outside, tires muffled on the snow, and the headlights moved across the ceiling, the engine a far-off, comforting sound of people going somewhere ordinary.

"You shouldn't miss tonight," said the Ripper.

"You work alone," Tuttle said. "You always did it alone."

The thing didn't move.

"Midnight," the Ripper said. "I want you at Miller's Court at midnight. We'll have a jolly time."

"What do you want with me? I'm no help to you."

"Come see," said the Ripper.

Tuttle felt a strange calm. Looking at death, he felt a strange calm.

"Something new," he whispered.

"I have to go and find a whore," the Ripper said, "I'll see you at midnight at

Miller's Court. Be punctual. Tomorrow you'll be famous."

"Something new," Tuttle said.

"That's it, boss."

"You've done a double before."

"That I have."

The image was in Tuttle's head, vivid and real. He saw the Ripper's mind. Saw it calmly, for all the shrieks of horror that surrounded it, for all the fury and sickness that gave birth to it. He saw the Ripper's mind, a thousand thoughts rushing by, black and nasty, clawing at each other, moaning, laughing, sobbing—he saw the Ripper's mind, took from it the one image, the image that concerned him: Miller's Court, where Mary Kelly had been reduced to shapelessness nearly a hundred years ago. Miller's Court, and he, Tuttle, sitting on the ground, his innards spilled in the snow, on his shoulders a yet nameless woman's head, whose gutted body sat facing his, wearing his own grinning head, two grotesque things, unspeakably wrong, staring at each other, monstrosities. Something new. It was the coming morning he had seen.

And slowly, still smiling, having shared his mind, the Ripper turned and left, and the last thing was the edge of his cape, fluttering out the door like a quick rush of wings.

A half hour until his midnight appointment and not a sound.

Tuttle sat behind the counter, smoking the first cigar of his life. He rather liked it. Could have had more of this. A little brightness, now and again.

He hoped the woman with the baby would be all right. He thought of her warming the milk tomorrow morning, warming the milk he had given her for the baby, thinking of him. How happy she would be. Thinking of him, thinking of Tuttle, fondly, she would be happy.

Could have had more of this.

I believe, he thought, I was a better Tuttle this last day. Wasn't I? I was trying to be. A better Tuttle than any that came before. That girl warming the milk while he sat in Miller's Court. He would need a gentle thought, wherever he would be.

It was almost time to go.

Oh, boy, Tuttle thought. Oh, boy.

What should I wear? ("He was dressed in a light blue overcoat, the front of which was . . .") He would wear his scarf. He hated to have his ears cold. It would be a quiet, moody walk to Miller's Court. He thought of the single, lonely set of footprints he would leave in the snow. He would hear nothing but the crunch of his boots. Perhaps stick out his tongue and catch a snowflake.

His cigar had two puffs left. Perhaps three. Yes, he decided. He would go. He would go as soon as it went out.

I guess, he thought, I'm wearing what I'm wearing.

The bell jingled.

Tuttle turned his head.

There were three of them.

They were very big men. One had a blood red stripe painted down the middle of his face

They looked hungry. Ravenous.

Their eyes moved about the shop. Trying to get their bearings.

Three huge, wild-eyed men. Steaming furs around their shoulders.

Two remained by the door. The third stepped closer. He radiated heat, from somewhere deep inside.

"Where is he?" he asked, in an accent that sounded of harsh mountains.

Tuttle didn't move.

"We been sent," the painted man said.

Tuttle nodded. Most normal thing in the world. Thinking: Oh, Jack. Oh, Jack.

"Miller's Court," Tuttle said.

The giant gave no sign of acknowledgement. But a light appeared in his eyes, the light of a predator spotting a track.

He turned and led his companions from the shop, and the bell jingled happily. They stooped to pass under the door.

Tuttle sat for some time, until the last sound of the bell had faded, and there was the sound of a car outside, and a drunk singing as he went, and a snowplow coming, gears cranking, flashing orange lights. He sat until everything was silent. He looked at his cigar. There was one puff left. He took it. It was the best one yet.

When the sun came up, Tuttle opened the doors wide. The snow was bright enough to hurt his eyes, the sky a cold, clear blue. Everything was white and clean and cold and without tracks.

Tuttle carried the antique chair outside. He returned for the Japanese fan and placed it on top of the chair. He set the chair on fire and stood in the door, watching the flames with a placid face. A place in the country.

The street sweeper who passed carrying a snow shovel received a warm "Good Morning."

"Good morning to you!"

Yes, the country. Soon.

What a nice fire.

It was a better Tuttle that walked back into the shop, that opened windows and drapes. Before lunchtime, the dog returned. Lay down in a patch of sunlight to sleep, and when Tuttle approached to scratch him behind the ears, Wellington's tail wagged in anticipation.

* * *

11:16 pm

He opened his eyes. Gwenna Luna wasn't at the window. She sat across the room. She held a framed picture in her hand and was looking at it. Wilson recognized the picture of his sister.

He felt exhausted and empty. You were there. The moor, the inn, the laboratory. He had traveled with Nadoni's circus, he had spoken to Jack . . .

Gwenna Luna studied the picture of his sister as if it would tell her something.

Wilson watched the darkness outside, feeling nothing. A truck made a turn and its light cut across the empty parking lot. For one moment, it drew something from the blackness. Someone was standing there, at the edge of the lot, under the trees. The figure wore a red cloak with some sort of hood pulled over its head and it was looking in the direction of the window. He saw it only for a moment before the light was gone, plunging the apparition back into the night. He wondered, vaguely, what would have happened if Gwenna Luna had noticed it.

It had, he reminded himself, never been there at all.

"*You're like someone sinking in quicksand,*" *Wilson said.*

The girl put the picture back on his desk.

"*Dragging in the person who's trying to save you.*"

The figure in the red hood had never been there, had never been there looking towards his window.

Lots of things can come . . .

"*What I'm trying to do,*" *Gwenna Luna said,* "*is to make you see that there is such a thing as quicksand.*"

He shook his head.

"*I won't save you by indulging you,*" *he said.* "*No. There's just atoms, chemical reactions, measurable . . .*"

She watched him, let him go on.

"*There's a medication I'd like to try you on . . .,*" *he mumbled. He stopped himself, realizing how empty he sounded. He looked up at her.*

"*I can't help you, can I?*" *he said.*

"*No,*" *said the girl.*

"*Why did you come to me?*" *he asked.*

Gwenna Luna stood up. She put her hand on the notebook.

"*One more dream,*" *she said.* "*And I'll tell you.*"

88

She opened the book, and to lose himself in the drawings was a relief, because he couldn't quite come back to where he once had been.

WISHES THREE

I had a best friend once. Many years ago, at university. Our friendship was based on contrast. I've always been a realist, a man of facts. Benedict Dean was a dreamer. A lover of the fantastic.

I studied mathematics. He studied the saints, ancient languages unheard for thousands of years, the tales of natives around the fire. He was an eccentric, yes. But his conversation eased my mind, like a beautiful song.

You see, after a night of talking to Dean, a return to my studies, to orderly lines, was a joy. He refreshed me, reminded me of my purpose. It was my subjects, my studies that had brought mankind up and away from the fire. Dean's ancient mists made me see the joy and value of reason.

He was, people took great pleasure in pointing out to me, an odd duck to have for a friend. Tall, stooped, even when he was young. And always, always dressed in white, shining white. Dressed in white like some sort of a mad druid.

What was he, exactly? Did I ever know?

After we took our degrees, there followed, for both of us, a period of near poverty. In his case, it was cloaked in the comfort of philosophy. His interests lent a certain dignity to poverty, making it appear almost a choice. My case was different. My chosen field came with a certain ambition toward making it. Tutoring untalented children and being nearly penniless gnawed on me, I don't mind admitting it. There is a system to success. The world is an equation to be solved. Systems were my talent and my chosen ground. Yes, it gnawed on me, my inability to prosper. I couldn't hide in mysteries. My failure was a failure of fact.

Around this time Dean became apprenticed to a priest. Not a clear-minded Protestant or a Catholic, even. No, not for Benedict Dean. His man called himself John Chrysostomos and was said to be an escaped monk from Mount Athos—a mystic, a renegade whose book of speculations on the afterlife was burned by his abbot. In Spain, he was involved in a scandal concerning a madness that took the children of a small village . . . oh, Dean . . . how perfect for you . . . how you relished it, you, dressed in white, spending your nights in study with that old wizard.

Dean told me they were working on that great man's biography. And when it was finished, he said, the Old would return . . . something older than Mount Athos, older than the Christ. Much, much older than the first hideous fish crawling upon land . . .

To propagate the strange and ancient tenets of this life, they had established what they called an Institute of Religious Thought. They were, as far as I could tell, its only members. Their work was underwritten, in a haphazard sort of way, by a collection of old widows. They always seemed to find a widow when a bill came due. The innocence of Dean's religiosity was, with the first payment made by the first old lady, on the wane.

One day, he came to see me with a proposition to solve our economic misery altogether. There was nothing metaphysical at all in what he suggested. It was an opportunity, cold and clear as can be. In less exalted circles it would have been called an angle. Through his studies, Dean had become, as a matter of course, an expert on ancient books. And while on a visit to the seaside town of Burnstow—he traveled there with his priest, on what errand I don't know—while in Burnstow, he had found a book on a shelf in a small antiquarian shop. It was old, anyone could see that, and beautifully bound. The owner of the shop, thinking it 18th century and a sort of moral tract or missal, asked a full hundred and fifty pounds for it, trusting in its beautiful leather binding. Dean, knowing it to be 15th century and exceptional, at a glance put its worth at a hundred times that price.

He proposed to pool our meager resources to buy the thing and realize a tidy profit by re-selling it to a collector of his acquaintance. I saw at once the moral issue involved in taking advantage of the ignorance of the book's current owner. In my case, this didn't present a problem—it was business, an investment with a healthy return and devil take the hindmost. But to Dean, who always went on about the immortal soul? Would Saint Francis have conned a village bookseller?

"The seller gets the price he asked. That will make him happy. Some collector will get his prize at a reasonable rate. That will make him happy. You, Allan, establish yourself in business, another good thing. And, of course, the work I have taken on, the Life of Father Chrysostomos, the institute . . . that, that alone . . ."

Ah, it was his no longer, the pure, simple honesty of a child's faith. He was far down the road of true religion, where an absolute cause justifies business to be conducted at the sharp edge of a pirate's cutlass. Dean was, to my surprise, a rather pragmatic druid when it suited his mission. He and his Father Chrysostomos were well on their way to becoming a pair of masterful religious con men.

I asked him then: What was that book you found? Not a missal?

"The Dread Evocations Of Alban the Blind. A standard work of black magic. Printed in 1483, written two hundred years earlier, with the help, it is claimed, of a demon. Not a missal."

So, Dean and I went to Burnstow. In my pocket I carried seventy-five pounds, my entire fortune. The shop, in an undistinguished side street well back from the sea, was not a memorable place. It had a modern store front of new windows, bargain bins with books left behind by tourists. A shelf held souvenirs and books on local attractions, of which bracing winds and sea birds seemed to be the chief ones. And then there was a glass case containing a few gaudy nineteenth century editions that really didn't need to be locked away at all. They were more interesting to a decorator than to a collector. Our book was in that case, unmistakable. It was smaller than I'd expected. It had a leather binding the color of . . .

Well, blood.

Dean never lied, but he made a face that made clear he considered the price outrageous but had his weak spot touched by the beauty of the thing. The bookseller, who was an old, kind man and not used to hard bargaining, held the door for us when we left and thanked us and I thought, with a thrill, that the plan had worked, the plan had worked.

Whose plan was it?

We were on our way back to the train station, in high spirits. We were, I remember, like we'd been at school. There's something in the human mind that makes this the most delicious of moods—a slight wrong successfully committed, nothing too serious, only enough to make you feel free, daring, a breaker of rules. Our ill-gotten gains felt like a sign of favor from the Gods, who, apparently, liked our pluck. The Gods, it seems, like their spirited, naughty children best.

We almost ran all the way to the station, laughing, and when we got there we collapsed on a bench and examined our prize. I took the book out of its shopping bag and handed it to Dean and he opened it.

A small piece of paper fell from the pages. Dean caught it and examined it. His face was thoughtful. He didn't throw it away. He studied it rather than the book. He handed it to me. The paper was clearly much later than our prize. It was a piece of ordinary notepaper, faded, the top jagged. On it, written in a clear hand that may have been a woman's, was this:

"This contract do I make
with both of you who found me:
The first of wishes three is yours, to do with as you please.
Mine to fulfill for you.
The second wish of three is yours, to do with as you please,
Mine to fulfill for you.
But mark:
The third wish also shall be yours,
Mine to fulfill for you.
But payment due thereafter.
Your blood and bones.
Your blood and bones.
For me, to do with as I please.
Your bloody bones, your bloody bones,
Your lovely, bloody bones."

On the back of the paper were written, in a quite different hand—a rather wild, clumsy one—the words:

"Three for each of ye! Hurrah!"

I made jokes about it, I remember—critiqued the poetry rather savagely, speculated on the store owner's ambitions as the Burnstow Bard. But I noticed that, somehow, the paper had spoiled Dean's mood. Not that its contents troubled him, I mean, it was clearly written for children, some game . . ., but it was as if his mind had found in it something it couldn't yet name and he was preoccupied and silent in the half hour we still had to wait for our train.

I found his silence oppressive. And there was something else—an uncertainty that the paper with its spidery writing and its blocky scrawl had produced in me. So, I talked. I joked. All to delay the moment when I had to admit to myself that uncertainty was not what I was feeling at all but rather a nameless, inexplicable dread.

"Dean, I swear I'm dying of thirst, and me a rich man . . . Do you have any change, by any chance? I wish we'd talked that man down to a hundred and forty, we could have a cup of coffee now . . . Hey, Dean, what are you in such a mood about? What do you mean you don't know?"

I talked and joked and chattered and the train came and we found our seats and still I talked.

He snapped at me. What he said was: "I wish you'd just shut up for an hour."

So, I curled up sulkily and went to sleep. I woke up again when the train reached London. And we got off the train and walked through the station, and only when we were in the street and it was time for us to separate did Dean stop. He put his hand in his pocket. And he pulled out something and showed it to me. "Look," he said.

It was a ten-pound note.

I asked him if it had gotten stuck in his pocket. He looked so solemn. He looked like he was in the presence of some miracle.

"We miscounted," I said. "Or he made a mistake with the change, he—"

"You said it," said Dean.

"I said what?"

"I wish we'd talked that man down to a hundred and forty, we could have a cup of coffee now . . ."

I still didn't quite get what he meant, so he pulled out that faded bit of note-paper.

The first of wishes three is yours, to do with as you please.
Mine to fulfill for you.

Three for each of ye. Hurrah.

"Oh, no," I said. "If only I'd known my powers, three wishes a man and I have to waste one on . . ."

He wasn't laughing.

"I did it, too," he said.

"Did what?"

"I wish you'd just shut up for an hour."

Your bloody bones, your bloody bones,
Your lovely, bloody bones.

"How long were you asleep on the train?" he asked me.

"About an hour—oh, come on!"

He had in his eyes the light of a mystic. He held that grubby piece of paper like the holy host.

"Come on," I said. "A couple of coincidences. It happens all the time!"

He held out that paper to me and I read the beginning of it again:

This contract do I make
With both of you that found me

"How," Dean asked, "did it know there are two of us?"

That was, apparently, the thing Dean had been thinking about. The odd, remarkable thing he couldn't put his finger on. The light of the mystic . . . you see, he was born to believe in strange things. But I thought I also saw, now, in his eye, a touch of greed.

We left each other then. He seemed too full of his absurd notions to bear my company; he had to be alone with his idea. This suited me. He puzzled and alarmed me in these inspired moods. I was, seeing him like that, not entirely sure if I hadn't been blind and, for all those years, the friend of a madman.

We agreed to meet the next day in a café. We'd both sleep on things. But as we parted, he did ask me for one favor: He wanted me to refrain, just for him, from making any sort of wish at all. It was absurd, of course. But I complied. Because to try the thing would have implied something like credence.

Our meeting the next day was not a success. Sleep had settled my mind firmly and upon waking it had been clear to me that there was nothing in our adventure but an anecdote. The morning light dispelled my dread, a dread that I now thought back on with a certain amount of embarrassment. But when I saw Dean waiting for me at the café, it was at once clear to me that his visionary mood was still upon him and had, in fact, increased.

He was set aflame by what had happened and all the implications it bore on our old conflict of reason and faith. I never felt the gulf between us more deeply than I did at that moment. Fantastical, childish madness. Where he had once been the contrast that made my reason shine, he was now triumphant. He wanted me to strike my colors. He was convinced that, at last, I had been vanquished.

97

"All right," he said. "If you don't take it on faith . . . experiment. It's what you men of science do, isn't it? Wish for something."

"We don't," I said, "need to experiment. Not on this. I urge you to stop this insanity."

I looked into his shining, eager eyes and I knew that this was the end of our friendship. And he looked into mine and saw my disbelief, and he knew it was the end, too. We'd reached a gulf too wide to bridge. And he leaned close to me and said, slowly: "I wish for Father Chrysostomos' Institute of Religious Thought . . . a wild success, renown and followers . . . with me to lead it."

And then he left me.

I waited.

There was a small story in the papers the next week, about Chrysostomos. Another the week after that: a woman said she had been healed. A man, after his child was lost and found, made a donation of twenty thousand pounds because Chrysostomos had prayed her back. After a month, the Institute of Religious Thought moved into a larger space. You couldn't see the holy man without an appointment, and within a year their meetings drew thousands—the papers wrote about a new spiritualism in uncertain times.

I watched. I watched the institute's rise . . .

There was never a word from Dean or one from me to him. The money from the book was long gone, and my hard times began again. It was absurd, I'd fallen asleep on the train . . . faith, nothing but faith, was that how it worked, he believed in it? Did faith, supported by the early coincidences on the train and the words found in that ancient book, have the power to make such things happen?

I watched and waited and starved. Dean prospered. I saw him, in the papers, always dressed in shining white.

One night, two years after having seen Dean for the last time, I got drunk and, standing by a river bank under a beautiful moon I said aloud: "I wish for a million pounds, half in cash and half in papers netting fifteen percent annually." And then I threw up and went home and to bed.

It must have been intentional. The clichéd banality with which the wish was fulfilled. The very next morning I received a call. An inheritance from an unknown uncle in Australia. The fortune amounted to a million pounds, half in cash and half invested so they would provide a safe annual return of fifteen percent. A distant uncle—I could feel the contempt in it. Someone was making a point. The fortune had been thrown at me like a coin at a once-proud beggar, the banal story making clear that throwing it hadn't even required the faintest effort.

There was a short notice in the paper about my inheritance. The day after its appearance I received a note from Dean written on fine letterhead paper of the Chrysostomos Institute. There was just one, gloating sentence: "Profess your faith."

I professed it, I suppose, in my own way. I was now rid of all material worries. I was allowed seclusion. Of that ominous fortune, I used only what I needed to live. I ceased going out or seeing people or taking any part in the world at all. There was a fear that paralyzed me. I felt, now, the clear, bright and rational world I knew to be surrounded by an endless, unknown blackness. And if you dropped a stone into that blackness, you'd never hear a sound.

In my seclusion there was only one thing that still had my obsessive attention: I followed, every day, the rise of Dean's institute—its publications, its conferences, pronouncements . . . all the time fearing . . . fearing . . . well, this:

The third wish also shall be yours . . .
But payment due thereafter . . .

About six months after I received my fortune, a well-known journalist, Carl Hickock, a feared progressive muckraker, wrote a small, scathing piece questioning certain business practices of the Chrysostomos Institute. Their lawyers, unwisely, tried to have the story suppressed. This ignited Hickock's journalistic bloodlust. Not a week now passed without another expose. He wrote about Chrysostomos' character, questionable investments, famous healings revealed as frauds. He wrote about real estate schemes, kickbacks, grants of public money. He wrote until I could see him drawing blood, doing real damage. And I knew Dean, and I knew about his faith and about the pirate's cutlass. And I thought: "Take care . . ." because I knew Dean had a weapon, and I knew how terrible a weapon it was.

It didn't take long. "Carl Hickock enters hospital," I read. "Mystery ailment." There was a picture of the man in his hospital bed. Marked by death, his eyes huge and mystified by what was happening to him and full of horror. He died within a week, and his illness never had a name.

Dean came to see me. After . . . he killed Hickock. Three years since I'd seen my friend. There was a knock on my door, late. When I opened, he slipped in like a ghost. Dean, dressed in white still, but changed, how changed. Horror changes people.

He never sat down but stood in the middle of the room in sort of a crouch, ready to spring. His eyes were mad.

"I did it," he says. His first words to me.

"I know you did."

"It wants my bones now."

"Who? Who wants your bones?"

"It's small," he says. "It's not an insect, exactly. But it's like an insect, somehow. It moves like it isn't used to things here, like it's from another place. Oh, have you ever seen an insect the size of a dog?"

"Where is this thing?" I asked him. "Where did you see it?"

He turned around then, and I had my answer.

"For the love of . . .," he paused there. God's love wasn't a certainty anymore. "Never make the third. It's like an insect but it's covered in hair."

And then he froze, turned his head.

"Was that a sound?"

And before I could stop him, he had run off and I was alone and I thought, all night, about how, in the extremity of his terror, he had come to warn me.

They found him the next day. There being no family, they called me to identify him. Which was not easy to do. Every single bone in his body had been broken, even the bones of his face. A slow death, like being broken on the wheel. I thought that it had probably taken a very long time until he had stopped moving entirely. They had there, at the morgue, the shredded clothes he had been wearing. I took away one scrap, I don't know why. Dean, always dressed in shining white, poor Dean, always dressed in white. So red.

Now my own horror began.

At the funeral, I threw the piece of paper with the poem into the open grave. Let it be buried with him. Let it be the end. My life continued quiet and withdrawn, dedicated to Dean's warning and example, dedicated, simply, to never uttering, under any circumstances, the words: "I wish . . ."

I came home one night. I didn't turn on the light as I walked up the stairs to my bedroom. When I reached the landing at the top, I heard, close, just behind my ear, a voice. It cleared its throat. Like an impatient man. And I was brought to a stop, stood there for a full half hour, stood there paralyzed by that sound and a strong, almost palpable feeling of malignance. Impatience. Malignance.

It was in a market place, full light of day, that it happened next. An old man accosted me. He held up a box of lottery tickets.
"No, thank you."
"Make a wish," he said.
That startled me, and I looked at him. His eyes were strange.
"Make a wish already, damn you" he said. "Like your friend."
I ran from him. Had I heard him right? His eyes had been an insect's eyes.

At night, my phone rang.
"Hello?"
Nothing.
"Hello?"
"Why haven't you made it?"
"I will not . . . there was nothing saying . . . I didn't agree to make three . . ."
"Do you know who he is?"
"Who? Who are you talking about?"
"What if I told you he was the devil?"
"I will not make a wish, I didn't agree to that, there is nothing in it . . ."
"He's the devil."
"I will not, and as long as I don't there is nothing . . . that was not the agreement . . ."
After a while I hung up, not sure how long I'd waited with the silent phone

pressed to my ear.

It moved in a strange way, Dean had said . . .

At night, I walked the city. I could not be at home, oppressed by the impatient presence that never left me now. Only towards morning, exhausted, did I turn into my street. When I approached my house, I saw a light in my upstairs window. It was my bedroom that was illuminated. When I got closer, I saw a dark, roundish form outlined in the window, looking out. It was a strange form, a cat perhaps, or a dog. I had no cat and I had no dog. It waited there, motionless, and I got closer, close enough to see, and then it turned and looked straight down at me.

It was a black, hairy thing with a segmented body and thin arms that moved like a wasp's, playing madly against the window pane. As it turned to me, all fell into place, and I saw where the eyes were, the dead insect's eyes, and where the mouth was, the strange, pincer-like mouth. It all fell into place in a moment and it jumped down from the window sill where it had been crouching and I knew that it hurried, in strange, awkward movements, downstairs to meet me.

I ran and I didn't stop, and I knew I could never come home again. At last, I remembered the one place I could go. There was only one man who . . . perhaps . . . perhaps . . . only one man to see . . .

I found the institute and, by using poor Dean's name and my connection to him, I got a message delivered and, a moment later, admission. A young, well-dressed man took me up to the fourteenth floor, looking at me suspiciously. And then I was in the presence of Father John Chrysostomos.

He waited for me in a conference room, in a leather chair behind a long table. Behind him, through the windows, I could see the city and the heavens. He wasn't dressed in white, as Dean had been and as I had pictured him always. He wore a modern, dark suit. But his face was ancient and like that of a priest dead for centuries, smelling of roses and kept in a glass coffin. He looked at me with interest and pity.

"You're the friend," he said. "Poor Benedict's friend. You're the other one."

"Yes."

"It's come for you."

"I never made the final wish! The agreement was for three—I stopped, I never . . . I never . . ."

"Those were the terms, were they?" the old priest said. Then he thought for a very long time, and I watched the clouds go by behind him.

"You have to understand," he said, "that this is the infinite."

The clouds covered the city, and we were alone in the heavens.

"Poor Benedict," said the priest, "He believed in prayer, sacred texts, study, religion . . . what a child he was, thinking it could be contained. You, on the other hand, believed in ignoring it altogether, believed in facts and figures. What arrogance . . . Terms, agreements, with whom? What do you want now? A judge? A referee? I've lived for two hundred and twenty years. And what I can tell you is this: in dealing with the infinite, you sit and stare at terrible beauty. There is only feeling, and awe. There's only a beautiful, dreadful music. Only hope for one thing. That the infinite, whatever it is, doesn't ever take any notice of you. Because it needs no terms with you, and if you want an explanation go and explain the works of Bach to a worm."

"Help me," I said.

The priest answered: "How?"

And there was a quiet scuttling on the landing.

* * *

Witching hour

Wilson, seeing nothing, stared through the window at the darkness. The rational mind, face to face with the infinite. He didn't need to interpret the last dream.

"Quicksand . . .," he said softly.

He was surprised to find her close, crouched next to his chair.

"I think," she said, "I may have been here too long. I think maybe I'm out of time."

He shook his head, not sure he understood. He remembered, vaguely, a figure in a red hood.

He looked at her and understood her less and less.

"Help," he said and she nodded, eagerly. He understood her less and less and they had, in that way, reached an agreement.

"Help," she said, still caressing that word.

"But why?" Wilson cried. "I can't help you; I can't do anything for you. Why come here, why me? Why show me these dreams? If you're out of time, if someone's after you—why don't you go, why show me all of this?"

"Don't you remember my plan?" the girl asked.

"Your plan?"

She nodded, childlike seriousness.

She had, the entire night, followed it.

"I had to show you the dreams."

"But why? I can't save you from your demons."

"Maybe I'm here to save you," she said.

"What do you mean?" Wilson whispered.

He had a notion of what she meant. He was beginning to understand. And the fear he had dreamed slowly entered the room.

"I had," said Gwenna Luna, "a dream about you."

"A dream about me . . .," he said.

"It was the same as the others. It was one of those that aren't dreams."

"But nothing . . .," Wilson said, "Nothing has happened to me."

"I know," said the girl. "That's just the thing. You're alive. It hasn't happened. That's the first time. You see what that means?"

There was such a need in her eyes.

"If I can save you . . ."

Wilson whispered: "Help."

"Yes," she said, "Help . . ."

"What," Wilson whispered, "did you dream?"

She hesitated. He could see how much it meant and that she didn't want to make a mistake, didn't want to chance it.

"Don't go to London," she said. "I thought if I showed you the dreams, you would listen to me. Do not go to London. Don't go. It happens there . . ."

She moved her hand across her throat, a cutting motion.

"Please . . ."

London, he thought, London.

He was lost in her eyes, that desperate need.

He was lost in her eyes.

That was their last moment together.

She turned to the window.

He watched her face change.

"Oh, no," he said, seeing her face change.

And the window shattered.

There was a howl, a voice, not human, and Wilson rose, saw a flash of red, and Gwenna Luna jumped on the desk, snatched up her notebook, just as a thin, yellowish arm was thrust through the broken glass and a hand that carried claws grabbed for her blindly, got a hold of her ankle and pulled on her with frightening strength.

Wilson stood against the wall, didn't know how he had gotten there, saw the girl fall, saw her dragged towards the window, saw the face there, a mask under long, flowing hair, a face of skull-like thinness.

With her free hand, the one not holding the girl, the woman outside held an old, rusty knife, brought it down, breaking off jagged pieces of glass, brought it down and rammed it into Gwenna Luna's leg, just above the ankle.

Wilson screamed, and for a moment the woman turned to him, and her eyes were on him and he screamed again because it was unbearable.

He saw Gwenna Luna reach into her bag, saw her bring something out—it looked like dust, a fistful of dirt—and she threw it, threw it at the thing in the window, yelling words that were ancient power. There was that scream again, and he saw the girl released, jumping from the table with uncanny grace, saw the knife slash blindly, once, then the thing withdrawing from the window, wailing as if wounded, disappearing into the dark . . .

But the dark was his already: he was falling again, the dark was everywhere, and

105

all was silent and he couldn't see Gwenna Luna anymore and he didn't know anything else. And he was, as he fell, desperately sorry that she was gone.

He was on his office couch, and it was morning. He sat up. Wilson realized that he was cold. He turned his head. The window was broken. That, then, had happened.

It was pure function, his body going through steps without his actual presence. He called the building security office, taped a piece of cardboard over the shattered window. Drove home, past the billboards, the gas stations. He would think again when he woke up. He slipped into bed and pulled the cover over his head.

There was, he remembered just before vanishing into sleep, a taxi ordered for tomorrow at ten.

The next morning, she was a ghost in his mind. He got up, showered, shaved. NPR Morning Edition. He was in his house and, of course, none of it had been real. The girl, yes.

"Gwenna Luna," he said aloud. He had read of cases like it, patients with visions so strong they infected their doctor, psychotic suggestions so utterly convincing . . .

None of it had been real . . .

He stood looking at himself in the mirror.

A taxi had been ordered for ten.

He looked over to the dining room table where the conference packet waited. Program, ticket, registration.

"London Mind Week"

London.

A taxi had been ordered for ten.

"Why have you come to me?"

"If I can help you . . ."

"Help . . ."

That awful need . . .

He still stood there, staring at the man in the mirror, when the taxi to the airport blew its horn outside.

The day was windy and the beach deserted. The restaurant by the pier was closed. But the girl had come for the payphone in front of the restaurant, which was still operational. She came up to it, walking with a limp. Took down the receiver. She put in several quarters but *waited for a while before dialing.*

"Good morning, Doctor August Wilson's office."

"Is Doctor Wilson in, please?"

Her voice sounded very young. She spoke fast and didn't trust it to say anything more.

"No, he's not in the office this week."

She bit down on the piercing in her lip.

"Is he . . . did he go to London?"

A wave crashed onto the beach behind her. The last wave, she thought, before she'd know.

"London? No, he didn't go to London. Dr. Wilson went to see his sister," said the voice on the phone. "He canceled London."

The girl stood for a while, holding the receiver to her ear.

Then she hung up.

The next wave came in behind her.

Gone to see his sister . . .

A better Tuttle . . .

The next wave came.

The next.

"Bam," Gwenna Luna said softly. "Good witch."

She stayed there, for a while.

So light.

She remembered she had to keep moving.

Adjusted her bag: Home Savings.

She walked away, down the beach, along the very edge of firm ground.

Guenther Primig was born in Austria and emigrated to Los Angeles, where he lived for 17 years. His supernatural fiction has appeared in many magazines and the anthology Shades of Darkness (Ash Tree Press). He lives in Berlin. This is his first book.

THE DEAD DON'T REST

THE GRAVEYARD
OF GWENNA LUNA

New Book Coming Soon!

Made in the USA
Middletown, DE
22 September 2020

19966506R00071